THE
DECISION

Vincent N. Scialo

authorHOUSE®

AuthorHouse™
1663 Liberty Drive
Bloomington, IN 47403
www.authorhouse.com
Phone: 1 (800) 839-8640

Published by AuthorHouse   07/25/2017

ISBN: 978-1-5246-9571-2 (sc)
ISBN: 978-1-5246-9570-5 (e)

DEDICATION

As I have done in the previous six books, I will once again praise those who have continued to offer me guidance, strength and support.

To Jen, my wife and life-long partner, who has stuck by my side through every imaginable obstacle that has crossed our paths. You continually raise me up to new heights that with only you can I accomplish them. I love you today as much as I loved you yesterday and will love you even more tomorrow.

To Marissa, my beautiful newly married daughter. May your life with Harry be blessed with love, showered with happiness and wished for continued health. Together you two compliment one another in ways that others could only hope for. You have proven to be a strong business owner with great potential to strive far. I love you today, tomorrow and always.

To Harry, my new son-in-law, who offers much support and is always there to help you out when needed. Your love, for my daughter is as clear as day, deep as the ocean, constant and what any father could hope for. I only wish the same for your daughter Stephanie one day.

To Jeff, my driven son. Hold onto your dreams, reach for the stars and continue your path to Kettle Corn stardom. You have the determination to make your success bigger than you can imagine. As a father no one could love a son as much as I love you.

To Kathy Zullo, who has again edited my book a big heartfelt thank you. As if she had a choice. Along with her husband Tony, Jen and I think of you as our good friends and enjoy your company whenever we get together.

And lastly to my faithful readers who constantly ask and urge me on to continue to write these stories. I thank you all and look forward to hearing your feedback. Many friends and family have made appearances one way or another in this book. Please forgive me for what I may or may not have done with your character. Some of you have been asking for years to be in one of my books. So please remember, be careful what you wished for.

God Bless and Thanks.

Part I

THE DISCOVERY

1

"Will you two lovebirds either get a room or better still wait another ten minutes, because according to the GPS that's how long until we get to the cabin," Meghan said jokingly as she peered into the visor mirror from the passenger front seat of the 2007 GMC Yukon.

"We've only been married less than six months yet, so can you cut us some slack? Wouldn't hurt to loosen those lips on Cole every now and then in the company of others. Hint, hint," snipped backed Danielle as she laughed at the same time.

"I swear if we haven't been friends since grammar school I would have written you off a long time ago. We're not into public displays of affection. Isn't that right honeybunny?," asked Meghan as she looked over at her husband Cole, as he drove.

"Whatever you say dear. As the old expression says, 'you can lead a horse to water but you can't make it drink'," snickered Cole.

"Oh, is that how you feel? So, let me get this straight. If I or better yet if you were to make advances openly in public, I should be more than willing to conform to your lewd outbursts," Meghan said as she lightly slapped Cole on his arm.

"Yikes, can everyone chill out? We can all do whatever we want once we reach the cabin. We can have a friggin' orgy if we like," said Matt from the middle row of the Yukon.

"Oh really, and just whose brilliant idea would that be to instigate this free for all? I hope I didn't just hear MY husband utter those words," answered Kimberly from the seat next to him.

"Alright, alright. We give up. No more foreplay until we hit the cabin. Promise! Just how long did you say again Meghan?" questioned Freddie.

Meghan looked down again at the Yukon's GPS map and stated, "Says we've been driving almost 4 hours and 20 minutes, should be there shortly."

The three couples had left Bellmore, Long Island on a late Friday afternoon after they all had cleared their schedules for the three-day ski weekend celebrating Martin Luther King's birthday, giving them Monday off as well. It wasn't easy for them all to do, but Meghan, being the most organized of the group, arranged the whole weekend. They were renting a log cabin on 650 acres of land, owned by an old man, whose name was Hector Skeeve, who also had another place of his own a few miles down the road. It was a three- bedroom cabin with a master bedroom with its own private bathroom and two smaller bedrooms that shared the bathroom in the hall. One of the bedrooms had a full-sized bed while the other room had bunkbeds. Since Meghan planned the trip she called first dibs on the master bedroom for herself and Cole. Kimberly and Danielle played rock, paper, scissors for the room with the full-sized bed and as luck had it Kimberly and Matt won. Danielle and Freddie, although the newlyweds of the bunch, would have to make do with bunkbeds, even though Freddie insisted that he was very capable of having sex anywhere, bunkbeds or not. Meghan did some research on which mountain had many green trails which were easiest for her and the other girls. Mount Snow in Vermont was by far the most family friendly ski mountain closest to them in Vermont. Cole and Matt, owned their own skis and were expert skiers. They wanted to ski outside of New York for a change of pace. Meghan was able to find the log cabin through Craig's list at a steal for the three nights. The lift tickets were a different story since it was a holiday weekend and no offers for a cheaper rate were available. All in all, each couple needed the break from their daily routines for the great outdoors and the snow-covered slopes that awaited them. The girls and Cole all went to grammar school together starting at Winthrop and finishing at John F. Kennedy High School in Bellmore. Danielle, Kimberly and Meghan met in the third grade while Cole was a grade ahead of them. Meghan and Kimberly lived just three blocks from one another. Cole was more north of Sunrise highway and Danielle lived closer to Newbridge Park. They remained friends throughout high school and college. The girls were all twenty-eight while Cole was just a few short months from his thirtieth birthday. Cole and Kimberly went to Cortland college upstate, while Danielle and Meghan went to Nassau Community college.

Danielle graduated with an associates of arts degree and went on to become a beautician and now worked at a hair salon on Merrick Road in Merrick. Meghan received her associates degree in science and went on to Queens College to finish her Bachelor's Degree. She was an Administrative Assistant at an Adult Day Health Care facility in Cold Spring Hills in Woodbury. All three girls were different in appearance. Meghan had curly shoulder length blonde hair and brown eyes with a height of 5' 7". Kimberly had short jet black hair with eyes as blue as the sky. Kimberly was the tallest of the three friends at 5'10". Danielle, on the other hand, had eyes that were green like a cat and long straight brown hair. She was the shortest of the girls at 5'4". The three of them were all fitness gurus and belonged to the newly opened Crunch fitness behind the Bellmore train station. Although the gym was close for both Meghan and Danielle, Kimberly would go either before or after work on her way to or from home. Meghan and Cole dated while she was in 11th grade and he was a senior and were married shortly after graduating college. They bought a house not too far from both their parents' homes on St. Marks Place north of Sunrise Highway. Cole became a lawyer after graduating and passing the bar. Cole was a strapping 6'2" with a swimmer's physique. Even his brown hair style was clean cut with very short sideburns. His eyes were the color of the Caribbean ocean that reflected the color of light blue when the sun shone down upon it. Although he didn't own his own firm, he was on his way up the corporate ladder in the law firm he worked for. He and Meghan married in the spring of 2013 and were approaching their fourth wedding anniversary. They had been trying to start a family for two years to no avail. The stress and disappointment was one of the reasons for the 3-day ski weekend. It would help to take their mind off things and while away they planned to relax and try again. The fact that they also owed an exhorbitant amount of money for his student loans just increased their level of stress. Cole's parents weren't able to help out with expenses beyond his four-year degree.

Cole had just made the final turn off the main road and they were now heading down a pitch black road covered with icy spots on the winding lane to the cabin.

"Cole A. Maercker, please slow down and look straight ahead. The last thing we need to do is skid out on this trail and wind up in a ditch," Meghan said nervously as she glared through the front windshield of the car.

"I've got this baby. Don't worry yourself. You'll make yourself sick. Besides it should be right around that last bend ahead. Now, stop straining your neck by leaning forward like an Ostrich and sit back and let me handle this," answered Cole.

"An Ostrich, now that's one I have never heard of. Awesome analogy," chuckled Matt from the back.

Kimberly shot back at her husband of two years, "Meghan's right. These road conditions are horrendous. It hasn't stopped snowing in the last two hours of our drive up here."

"Totally awesome. Think of how great the slopes will be this weekend. Rad man, rad," bellowed Matt once again. Matt Quigley was the oldest of the three couples at 32 years old. He was originally from the west coast of San Diego who came to school on the east coast after losing both his parents to cancer six months apart when he was fourteen years old.

His father's sister was never married and raised him since he was their only child. She lived in West Babylon which was only minutes from Gilgo beach and in Matt's way to deal with losing his parents, took up surfing to grieve in his own way. The solace of the waves and the calmness of the ocean, eventually became his passion and led him to compete in many surfing tournaments on Long Island over the summer months. With a lean build along with his golden shaggy locks and blue eyes, he was the true version of a Californian surfer dude. At 6' tall and with his chiseled features he could have been a male model on any Manhattan runway. Instead he chose the life of a surfer with lifeguarding in the summer and bartending at various restaurants during the winter months. Matt met Kimberly a few years before while he was a lifeguard at Point Lookout Beach who rescued her after she got caught up in a rip tide. They started dating shortly afterwards and were married a year and a half after they met. Kimberly wanted so much more of him but had settled on the fact that his life ambitions were not as high as she had hoped. They were currently living with his Aunt Mary in West Babylon with hopes of one day owning their own home. Kimberly was a paralegal who worked for a different law firm than Cole. Her job was right by Roosevelt Field Shopping Mall in Garden City. Once the girl who could easily go on a shopping spree at the spur of a moment, now had to think twice before stepping foot in the grandest of malls on Long Island. While she made a somewhat decent living as a paralegal, the income that Matt provided barely helped out since it was never consistent.

"Sorry guys but I have to side with the girls on this one. Even though you are driving this monster of a Yukon, there is no guarantee the tires can't lose traction on these icy roads," shouted Freddie from the last row in the truck.

Cole was next to speak, "Spoken like the true mechanic that you are. I will now take heed of this."

"Oh sure," smirked Meghan. "Listen to him but pay no mind to me and Kimberly. Nice Cole, Nice! See what fun I'll be later on when YOU want to make YOUR display of affection behind closed doors."

"Ah come on, you know he was listening to you as well," chimed in Freddie. "Just like he said with me being a mechanic and all. Add in the fact that I am, after all, the youngest of this wisest group and well, well la".

Freddie Torres, was two years younger than Danielle, and also the only non-Caucasian of the bunch. He was of Spanish descent and lived in Shirley in Suffolk County prior to meeting Danielle. Also like Matt and Kimberly, it was by chance that he and Danielle met. It was a hot summer afternoon about two years prior that Danielle and a couple of her co-worker girlfriends rented a house for a week in the Hamptons. On her drive out to the Hamptons on the Long Island Expressway near exit 70 in Manorville, her car started to overheat. It was a blistering 92 record high degrees for that day and her car was over ten years old. As she was unfamiliar with cars she did what any girl or person would do she pulled over and stood in front of her car with her arms crossed. What seemed like endless hours, though in actuality it was only a matter of minutes, not one person stopped to help her. Nowadays, everyone is so wrapped up in their own little worlds that no one takes the time to help a fellow motorist in distress. Add in the fact that every fellow human being has a cell phone and why bother to stop and there you have it. Just as she was about to call AAA, along came Freddie Torres, her knight in shining armor. Within five minutes he had added water to her radiator and a bit of antifreeze and she was good to go. Smitten instantly by her prettiness, Freddie offered to follow her to her final destination. Upon arriving at her rental house, before Meghan took mental notice, she had invited him in for a glass of wine. Although Danielle was only 5'4" Freddie was at least an inch or two shorter than her. Where she was lean, he was a bit more stocky and muscular. With dark eyes to match his dark hair, Danielle had never been attracted to such a guy with these type of features. She had always dated guys taller and more leaner than this man. But oddly enough she felt safe and protected just within his company the last couple of hours. Instead of spending the week with her co-worker girlfriends, she wound up spending almost every minute she could with Freddie. Since he worked in an auto shop 20 minutes further east than his family's house in Shirley, he was closer to head straight to the Hamptons after he finished up at work. While she did manage to soak up the sun during the day with the girls, at night she was not to be seen. She spent every evening in the company of Freddie, until she practically had to force him leave to get some shut eye before work the next morning. Even though they were complete opposites, somehow with their undying and relentless love for one another, just recently had them walking down the aisle. They currently resided in a one bedroom apartment in Massapequa Park. Freddie still made the hour drive to work each morning but didn't mind since being married to Danielle was all he cared about.

No sooner had Freddie made that snide remark and

Cole had slowed down to a controllable speed, a doe and two of her fawns had pranced straight into the road unaware of the Yukon heading straight for them. Cole noticed them first just as Meghan and Kimberly both let out high piercing screams making both Danielle and Freddie grab onto each other for the point of impact. The expression of a deer in the headlights took total effect as mother and babies froze still in the center of the road. If it weren't for Meghan's insistence that Cole slow down and the fact that the brakes on the Yukon were recently replaced, a collision was inevitable. With reflexes as fast as lightning and the precision of a drag race car driver, Cole avoided hitting the trio by inches. As soon as the Yukon came to a full skid stop, the mother along with her two fawns took flight into the dense brush.

"Holy mother of God! Did that just happen?," cried Meghan. "Holy, holy shit. Please tell me that didn't almost happen," again she cried.

Cole, shaken up, but trying his best not to show it replied, "Okay everyone, let's all take a deep breath and just thank our lucky stars we came out of this one with no scratches on us or this car. I can't afford to have this car totaled out right now. And, as much as I made fun of you Meghan, I'm glad you stuck to your guns about the speed."

"You can thank me too," said a badly shaken up Kimberly. "I was getting on your case as well."

"Damn dude that was close. I mean another six inches and forget about grandma getting run over by a reindeer," Matt stated as he reached forward with his hand and gently placed it on Cole's shoulder. "I mean what the fuck, where did they come from?" Matt continued.

Cole sat still and stiff as ever as he listened to them all

get their bearings again. Freddie and Danielle were entwined like a jigsaw puzzle which made Cole snap out of it. He then replied "Okay, time to get moving again. We are literally yards from the cabin according to the GPS. Everyone feeling better now? Let's put this behind us and have fun. It could have been a lot worse." He then smiled as he started to drive the Yukon again and said, "After all, from here on it should be smooth sailing," unaware of what was yet to come.

2

They all had calmed down as the Yukon made its way up the drive to stop in front of the log cabin. Meghan was the first to step out into the complete darkness, as she watched both Matt and Kimberly exit next. "Hey, hey, hey, can someone lift the seat so we can get out too?," asked Freddie from the last row of the SUV. "Nice of all of you to forget about us LOVEBIRDS," he laughed as he and Danielle had released their tight grip on one another.

"I guess if you put it that way, we have no choice," Matt said as he lifted the seat to make room for them to get out. As soon as the five of them were out, Cole shut off the engine and released the trunk latch so they could gather up their belongings.

"Is it me or does it seem eerily quiet out here? It's giving me the creeps," Kimberly said as she made her way to the back of the SUV. She stood at the back with her arms folded together as Cole started to unload their duffle bags and groceries to be brought inside.

Her husband Matt was the first to answer her, "Relax

baby, I got you covered and like the true surfer dude that you all like to refer to me as, COWABUNGA and chill!" No sooner had he said that statement, that all six of them forgot about Kimberly's eerie feelings moments ago, and started to crack up with laughter.

3

Meghan had just knelt and was searching under the back leg of the brown wicker rocking chair on the front porch, when her hand grazed the key. She picked it up and said in an excited tone, "Got it! That wasn't so hard. Listening to the old man over the phone made it sound like he had it hidden like the gold in Fort Knox." As she stood up she started to walk over to the front door of the cabin. Cole and the others followed each carrying their own duffle bag. Cole had slung Meghan's over his shoulder. All three guys each had a couple of white plastic bags with groceries that they brought along with them. They had planned to have most of their meals at the cabin and to bring sandwiches made from the cold cuts they had bought for lunch at the ski lodge. As Meghan inserted the key into the lock she simultaneously had her hand on the doorknob, when the door opened before she turned the key in the lock cylinder. "That's odd," she said. "I think the door was open," as she pushed the heavy wooden door and started to enter the cabin. "When I spoke to him, Mr. Skeeve had given me specific instructions on exactly where to find his key. Strange, really."

Matt was first to speak up from the bottom step, "Maybe you did open the lock. Your head is probably still in la la land after the near miss with those deer. Besides, I'm starving. Which one of you lovely ladies is cooking up that yummy London broil we got from Stop and Shop?"

Kimberly who was directly behind Matt pushed him lightly on the back and said, "Jesus, Matt. If it isn't about food or sex, you most certainly are lost. Oh, and heaven forbid I forgot to mention surfing. I don't know where I come in in the order of your priorities." Matt replied with a smirk, "But baby you're my number one!" Danielle and Freddie now made their way up the steps just as the other four entered the cabin.

Cole was first to speak, "Geez, its pitch black in here." He dropped his duffle bag near his feet and started to feel along the inside wall for a light switch. "Can't seem to find a switch. Meghan put your phone light on. This way at least we have some light to find a lamp or something." All six were now crowded in the front room of the cabin as Meghan took her phone out of her bra and played with the screen until a flashlight beam shone. Meghan was about to shine it on the wall inside the door, when suddenly the beam caught the silhouette of someone sitting on a couch. Kimberly screamed as she backed into Danielle forcing Danielle to scream too. Meghan shone it back on the figure again and also jumped back in surprise.

Sitting on the couch was an old man. He leaned over the side of the couch and with his arm outstretched turned on a lamp saying, "Sorry, I didn't mean to scare you all like that. I must have dozed off for a second. I thought I heard the engine of a car and was just about to turn on this light but you youngins are much faster than me. The name is Hector. Hector Skeeve. Which one of you ladies is Meghan Maercker?"

Meghan hesitated before answering. Never had she in all her years seen such a disfigured face. The old man looked like he was a burn victim. The whole right side of his face was discolored a deep purplish. What was left of his nose were barely the nostrils and even his lips looked flat on his face. The top of his head barely had any hair. Loose strands of gray stuck up in scattered places on his skull. With a tremble in her voice she answered Hector, "Oh, I'm….I'm the lady. I mean girl. I'm the lady girl," she stammered. "Oh, you know what I mean. My name is Meghan. And you, you must be Hec…Hector."

Noticing how surprised his wife was and how flustered she was becoming, Cole jumped in, "Honey, Mr. Skeeve just introduced himself. Pardon her, we just drove almost 5 hours and practically came face to face with a deer and her family in the road. I guess we weren't expecting you to be here in the cabin."

It took Hector nearly a full minute to brace his hand on the arm of the couch and push off to gain his balance to stand upright. As he did this he noticed six sets of eyes watching his every delicate move, "Yeah, well I did mean to be gone by the time y'all got here. We had a power outage and no electricity for a couple of darn hours early this morning. I figured I'd check to make sure the hot water heater had kicked back on for y'all. But then the snow started to come down real hard and as an old geezer of 87 years I didn't want to slip on my way out and break a hip. My place is about a mile down the road from this here cabin. Figured I'd wait out the storm and now look, I got to meet you all here." With his hand outstretched, he started to walk over to the group. Meghan noticed how lean and frail his body was.

His clothes hung loosely from his body. In a flannel shirt and worn out dungarees, he walked with a slight limp as he approached. Sensing the tension and witnessing how all six had taken a step back, Hector tried to lighten the mood, "It's the sight of these damn here clothes sagging off this old body of mine isn't it? Sorry if they're outdated. Didn't mean to frighten you."

Cole spoke up again, "No, sir not really it's just….." as he stopped mid-sentence.

"Oh, this face of mine. Been in an accident, well over fifty years or more now. I honestly don't even remember the year. Been so gosh darn long. Quite an eyesore huh? I reckon you can turn off your phone light or whatever that there contraption is y'all have on." Meghan was still in shock over his appearance and as she went to turn her phone around in her hands, she fumbled and dropped the phone to the floor. The old man again noticed how they all stood there frozen in place and went to bend over to retrieve the phone off the old wooden floor. As he was bending, he suddenly had a spasm or more of a Charlie horse and fell to the floor on his side, wincing in pain. No one did anything at first. Actually, for some strange reason the fall made Matt and Freddie start laughing. Kimberly as well as Danielle who only moments ago had screamed, joined in the laughter because they were so nervous. Sensing how this whole scene must have made the old man feel, Meghan quickly snapped out of her trance and knelt beside him as Cole did the same and started to lift him to place him on the couch. After he was seated, Hector frantically rubbed on his calf to stretch out his muscle. As gruesome as his face was previously, it was even more hideous when contorted in pain.

Meghan, once again took a step back and realizing how horrible this old man must be feeling tried to soften the blow by saying, "So sorry for my friends' behavior or should I say outburst. I don't know what came over them. Honestly guys, knock it off." The two couples looked at one another and had stopped laughing. Danielle still covered her mouth as she still let a couple of chuckles escape. "Is there anything I can get you? A glass of water or something?," Meghan asked. Cole started to head to the kitchen which was directly behind the living area they were in.

Hector more embarrassed that he fell over and less concerned about their laughter anymore replied, "No thank you ma'am." Trying to lighten the mood once again, he continued. "I'm not really thirsty but more hungry than anything else. I live alone and I don't cook for just myself. Not any fancy meals for sure. I could use a nice home-cooked meal. And from the looks of all those bags of food you got over by the door, I hope I wouldn't be imposing."

Kimberly and Danielle looked like a curveball had been thrown their way and they couldn't duck fast enough. A look of instant horror replaced their giggles from seconds before. Matt, the golden surfer boy, always fast on his feet answered for them all, "Dude, I mean sir. We weren't planning on eating in tonight. We were going to head to that sports bar down the road in West Dover near the ski resort. Maybe another time. I mean sorry and all but it isn't gonna happen tonight." Matt who never really went on like he was now continued to babble, "Only because like I said we......"

Kimberly who knew her husband could be harsh but not to this extent interrupted him. They had each managed to hurt this old man's feelings enough in one way or another and said as politely as she could "Don't mind my husband. It's just that we are all so exhausted from the drive up that none of us is really up to cooking a meal right now." You could see the guilt on all of their faces from the outright lie. Hector knew it was because of his appearance. They would not be able to sit down and eat a meal with him present at their table. He had experienced this throughout the years, time and time again and had hoped just maybe this lot of young folk from Long Island would or could be different. From the moment he fell and they started to laugh, even if it might have been nervous laughter, they were just like the rest he had come across over the decades.

Sensing it was his time to leave and feeling mortified by all that had happened in such a short time, he stood up as the charlie horse had since subsided and said, "I see. Roads are pretty bad out there but if you say so. After almost hitting a deer, I think you are a foolish bunch but it ain't up to me to pass judgement. Well then, now that's settled would you care for a tour of the rest of the cabin? The bedrooms and such?" And like six bumbling fools they all started to answer at once. You could barely make out who was saying what but the overall consensus was they didn't want this disfigured old man to stay a second longer than necessary.

Cole asked first, "Come to think of it. I didn't notice a pickup truck or car of any sort in the front of this cabin. How did you get here and what is your plan on leaving?"

Now it was the old man's turn to chuckle, "Y'all are a strange bunch. With y'all talking at once. Hardly able to make out what y'all were saying other than my time here is over. I thought that the Texans were a flaky bunch when I lived down south. They don't hold a candle to the bunch of you! And to answer your question…." He looked over at Cole. "I never did get all your names. Not that it matters anymore. I reckoned the roads were bad when I headed out this way to check on the place to make sure it was up to par for y'all. I took my snowmobile and came through the trails out back from this cabin straight to mine like I said is a mile or so down the road." He started to walk towards the kitchen which appeared to have a back door leading outside. As he passed by the three couples, he couldn't help to notice how relieved they were that he was leaving. Their body postures became more relaxed, even though they still didn't look directly at his mutilated face. Knowing that they still couldn't fathom an old man on a snowmobile in this type of weather, he bundled up his coat, hat and gloves left at the back door. Hector glanced over to them one last time and said, "Also a word to the wise. When you get ready to fire up that London broil later on tonight, make sure you all enjoy it real good." Adding one last statement that he knew would really leave them shell shocked he said, "I may be ugly and eighty seven years old, but I ain't dead yet." He then opened the back door and was out of sight in a few seconds at most. Next thing the group heard was the start of the snowmobile engine kick on and listened as the sound dimmed as he sped off into the snowy night.

4

Matt spoke first as they picked up their bags and headed toward the kitchen area, "Now that was some sick shit if I must say so myself. Friggin' scary-looking dude."

Danielle looked around, and with a deep sigh of relief after the old man had left, took in a deep breath and coughed, "Is it me or does it smell kinda stuffy in here. I mean look at this kitchen. These appliances must have been found by the side of the road. And you call this a kitchen table." The table was a matte white laminate with red vinyl sparkled with silver piping and buttons. The vinyl on two of the six chairs was worn and cracked and the white laminate had tinges of gray matted in. The refrigerator was also white but from years of not being properly cleaned, had a brownish tint to the outside. The stove was a cast iron black oven that easily dated back to the early 1900's. There was no dishwasher and a toaster oven that was so blackened you couldn't even make out the glass door. "I hope we will be able to cook our meals here," continued Danielle. "Not for nothing Meghan, but what were you thinking?"

Meghan, who had known Danielle most of their lives knew she could be a tad bit spoiled ignored her rude question and answered her anyway, "I guess that's what you get when you look for a place on Craig's list. I should have known especially since it was so cheap for the three nights. I tried to do the right thing for all of us. How Hector would even know how to put this place on Craig's list surprises me even more. He must have had someone help him."

Freddie spoke next. "I don't know who would be willing to sit down with that old man and that face of his. I mean he made Freddie Krueger look pretty. What was his last name? Skeeve like in I skeeve you?"

Meghan couldn't hold back and blasted into Freddie for his last comment, "Really, did you see how we all acted towards him. I feel sorry, no, horrible that we acted the way we did. Shame on us all. Imagine having to go through most of your life as disfigured as Hector. And what did we all do? We treated him like he was a leper. Couldn't get rid of the poor old man fast enough. He even knew we were bullshitting about going out for dinner. You heard what he said as he was leaving. And to even pick on his last name…!"

Cole, sensing that Meghan was on the verge of tears, because of her emotional distress with trying to start a family, and the fact that she was the most sensitive of the girls, put his arm around her and said, "I say we all take it easy and check out the rest of this place." The cabin was small compared to the outside. It consisted of a living room with a fireplace, the eat in kitchen and the three bedrooms with the two bathrooms. Off the living room which had a brown couch and two mismatched recliners with ottomans, there was an old 19" television and two lamps on end tables on both sides of the worn-out couch. The hardwood floor was in desperate need of a polishing but somehow with its rustic appeal suited the living room quite nicely. The mantel of the fireplace had a couple of old bronze statues of various animals. There was a bear, elk and reindeer all in various positions and poses covered with years of dust. The black bear was on its hind legs with claws outstretched while the reindeer grazed in the grass. The elk stood tall as if sensing danger from yards away. Although outdated, they each cast their own sense of calm to the comfort of the living room. There was a bundle of firewood stacked alongside the fireplace and more outside in a wood pile next to the cabin. Off the living room was a short hallway with shag carpeting from the 1960's early '70's. It was the color of grass so green that it looked like a strip of a lawn more than a hallway. Each bedroom had the same color green shag as the hall. The master bedroom consisted of a queen sized bed, two night tables and one four drawer dresser with a small mirror on top. The furniture was dark oak and the bedspread was a floral pattern that matched the curtains on the two windows. The master bathroom wasn't as bad as they might have expected. For some reason, it appeared to have been recently renovated with a modern sink, toilet and shower and tub. The other two bedrooms were more of an eyesore. Nothing in either of them matched and both the full-sized bed in the one room and the bunk beds in the other were from many years before. Again, like most of the other rooms, there were no light switches, only floor lamps in each corner of the room. The kitchen and two bathrooms were graced with a ceiling light fixture operated by an on/off switch. The six of them carried their duffle bags into their chosen rooms and advised one another that they would all meet in the kitchen to start to prepare dinner. On the menu for tonight was a hearty green salad, with mashed potatoes, corn and a juicy London broil. They also brought along three bottles of champagne, three bottle of both red and white wine and two 24 packs of beer. Danielle also insisted they bring along some liquor and juices. She managed to pack along Fireball cinnamon whiskey, Tito's vodka, Malibu rum and Rum Chatta to finish their assortment of alcohol. Recently at the local bar she frequented, she had a shot of fireball and rum chatta. It tasted just like cinnamon toast crunch cereal and she was hooked from that point on. Although you didn't quite taste the alcohol, which made it easier to pound down, after only a few shots, you felt the impact. The girls had each told their significant others to leave the bedroom as they had all concocted a little surprise for their husbands. As the guys were instructed to start the dinner preparation, as they each enjoyed cooking, the girls changed into matching pajamas. They wore matching off white one piece zippered pajamas with footsies. The print on each was of Frosty the Snowman in all types of poses. In some of the poses he held a broomstick, in others a pair of skis and the remainder he held a lantern outstretched in front of him. Printed in all different areas were separate words of jolly, holly, and hello dolly. Kimberly had seen them online at Spencer's gifts while Christmas shopping and purchased all three sets. She had given them to the girls on the hush with the intent of wearing them all at once to the surprise of their spouses. When they each had finished dressing, they poked their heads out of their bedroom doors. On the count of three, they raced out and down the hall like young school girls giggling all the while. With the laughter emanating down the hall, they had now gained their husbands attention as they curtsied upon their arrival.

Cole, Matt and Freddie each took one look at their wives and started laughing. "What the hell possessed you girls to buy them yet alone wear them?," Cole said as he had to catch his breath from belly laughing so hard. Danielle had just finished galloping down the hall with her long brown hair pulled back in a ponytail, neighing the whole time, making the guys burst out in laughter even more. Kimberly had spiked up her short black hair with gel and looked like a punk rocker. Meghan took her curly blonde hair, tied them in swirls and put them in pigtails. All three different appearances were quite amusing causing the guys to crack up even more.

Kimberly knew they looked none for the wary, "So, how do we look? Move over Princess Kate. You aren't the only one who knows how to make a fashion statement."

"You can say that again. No, better still, please don't. I think you girls should hit the slopes wearing those PJ's. You may even get your lift tickets for free," Matt said as he looked his wife Kimberly up and down. "I, for one, would let you ride the chairlift free all day just to see those footsies dangling in the air", he said again as he turned away from the imbedded image of his wife in Frosty garments. Just to get his goat even more, the girls all started to hop around like bunnies laughing as they went around him in circles. Upon his first chance at breaking through the circle, Matt made a quick leap between Danielle and Meghan. He headed clear away from them. Throwing his hands up in the air he lamented, "Now, I've seen enough. Why don't you girls fix the beverages as we finish the dinner. We somehow by the grace of God figured out how to work this dinosaur of a stove and it seems to be cooking the London broil quite nicely. Dinner shall be served in approximately twenty minutes tops." While Matt began to whip up the mashed potatoes, Cole had made an extra trip along with Freddie back outside to retrieve the large blue cooler. The cooler was filled with beer, white wine and champagne and kept on ice during the drive up to Vermont. They had since placed it in between the kitchen and living room providing easy access from both rooms. They placed the red wine and liquor bottles on the kitchen countertop and put the juices in the fridge. While Cole tended to the salad and corn, Freddie found places either in the refrigerator or cupboards for the remaining groceries they had brought along for the long weekend. Danielle had continued to gallop to garner some more laughs as she asked where they had placed the Fireball and Rum Chatta. She took a large pint glass out of one cabinet and preceded to wash it. Freddie had already placed some Palmolive soap and a sponge by the sink just as he had put the groceries in their designated areas. Meghan followed suit and took out some red solo cups for the shots.

Kimberly noticed there were some champagne glasses on the top shelf where most of the glassware was kept. At 5'10" she was the tallest of the girls and by pushing up on her tippy toes was able to pull six off the shelf. "Well, look what we have here. These champagne glasses look like real crystal," she stated as she tapped her nail on the rim to hear the soft ring of real crystal. "Amid this whole decrepit place we find crystal champagne flutes! Go figure. I'd say for that alone, we need to make a toast to a fun-filled ski weekend regardless of the rustic accommodations."

"Here, here!," chimed in Cole as he went over to the cooler to take out a bottle of the Korbel Brut Champagne. After quickly washing the flutes, she placed all six on the kitchen table. Cole twisted off the seal and slowly turned the cork, making only a slight popping sound as he handed over the bottle for Kimberly to pour.

Danielle held her hand over the closest flute and stopped Kimberly from pouring, "Wait, first let's do the cinnamon toast shots I made." She had already filled the red solo cups with her newest hot shot and passed a cup to each person. "Here's to a great ski weekend ahead. And may we all have the grandest of times out in the open pastures, breathing in only the freshest of air and…."

"We get it already. And may life offer us only good intentions and blah blah blah," retorted her husband Freddie as he picked up his red solo cup, tapped it against the others and downed his shot. "Yummy yummy for the tummy," he replied as he rubbed his not so flat stomach of his 5'2" frame. Of the three guys he was by far the shortest and darkest of the trio. Since all three girls had basically grown up together along with Cole, he sometimes felt like the outcast among the group. Cole had an in from the start and Matt was the blonde haired, blue-eyed surfer dude, with the golden tan year-round. Matt's looks alone made him appear to be an Adonis, which also added to Freddie's insecurity about his own physical and facial appearance. Danielle in the meantime had poured herself a larger shot of the remaining fireball and rum chatta and was instantly feeling giddy, having not eaten for most of the day. Having finished her own shot rather quickly, Kimberly started to pour the champagne into the flutes. She handed one glass to each of the group and raised her own glass. She was preparing to make a shorter toast than Danielle had attempted moments ago, when Danielle lost her grip on the flute and watched as it slipped from her fingers. The crystal flute hit the floor with such force that it shattered into what looked like a million tiny shards of glass.

Startled by her own clumsiness, Danielle reacted by saying, "Now look what I just did. I'm such a clumsy fool. I hope I ski better than I do holding a glass of champagne. No one move. I noticed a small pantry off the kitchen when I went to get the liquor before. I'm sure there must be a small dust pan in there or at least a broom to sweep these pieces up. Funny how a tiny incident like this can sober you right up. And I was just starting to get my buzz on." All the others continued to sip their champagne as Kimberly never made her toast. In the meantime, Matt checked on the London broil, as Cole, Meghan and Freddie watched Danielle walk toward the pantry. Danielle opened the door to the small pantry. The room itself was no larger than a clothes closet. It smelled even more stale than the rest of the house did. Holding her nose for the first few seconds she looked for a light switch of any sort. Hanging from the ceiling was a short white string attached to a single bulb at the top. She gently tugged on the string and a dim yellow glow from the bulb flashed on. Rummaging around in the pantry under the poor light that illuminated the room, she searched high and low for anything resembling a broom. There was fishing gear and a tackle box along with some old snow boots from the turn of the last century. There had to be at least two dozen empty mason jars scattered all over the three shelves along the wall. The opposite wall had coat hooks and each one of the six hooks had numerous coats and sweaters hung from them. There wasn't a single item of canned food or any type of food for that matter in what a pantry is used for. Getting more frustrated by the second, Danielle pushed away at shoeboxes on the floor and even got on her hands and knees to see if a dustpan may have been hidden deep behind this mass collection of waste. Just as she was about to give up hope of finding anything of any use, her hand brushed up against a duffle bag in the far-right corner of the pantry. Knowing that this couldn't contain a dust pan or broom, her curiosity got the best of her. She pulled at the handles of the duffle bag and watched as what looked like years of dust come flying off the top. The large bag was green and appeared to be from some sort of military service. The duffle bag was large enough to hold a small child. Danielle heaved once more until the bag was now right in front of her. Again, the dust swirled in the air circling around her. She sneezed twice and coughed even harder as she wiped her hands off on her Frosty the Snowman pajamas. Sensing this bag was even older than her, she gently tugged on the zipper trying not to rip it. As she pulled it open, her first glimpse was what looked like bundle upon bundle of what appeared to be stacked money. She instantly stuck her hand in the bag and pulled out a crisp stack of one hundred dollar bills all neatly arranged with each bill facing up. The stacks were covered in plastic as to only expose the both ends of the bills. Danielle quickly moved the other stacks to the side and saw that there were more stacks of hundreds. She couldn't imagine just how much was in this one large duffle bag. She plopped herself down on her butt, no longer caring whether or not she dirtied good old Frosty, and stared in amazement at her new found discovery.

5

No sooner had he gotten back to his tiny abode, Hector went directly to sleep. The mental exhaustion he just experienced from that group of vulgar people, left him drained and spent. Although it was an hour or so earlier than his normal bedtime, he hit the sack to call it an early night. It felt like only minutes that he had drifted off, when with a sudden jolt in his body, Hector Skeeve sprung up in his bed. A feeling of utter panic washed over him and he felt his whole entire body start to perspire. A vision appeared before his eyes and in it he saw a hand tug at the duffle bag of money. He felt it deep within his bones that the cursed money had been discovered. One of those six nasty people just thought they struck gold. Boy, were they in for a rude awakening. Hector wondered aloud just who of the bunch made the untimely discovery. He had hoped it was that short dumpy guy. Of the three couples, he looked at him with the most disgust. In actuality, it sent shivers up his spine with the hatred he had felt emanating toward him from that puny bit of a guy. Although Hector faced decades of unnatural stares and glances from strangers, most with either pity or disgust, he still couldn't believe the pure sense of evil some people possessed. Nowadays most strangers he walked past in the street would glimpse his face and quickly glance down at the pavement as they passed. Afraid if they stared too long, he may pass along his ugliness in their direction. Over the years, Hector managed to bear the fruits of his fellow humankind bitterness and unkindness to him, but tonight was the icing on the cake. The duffle bag containing almost two million dollars in cash had been hidden away for many years. So many years he finally lost count. There was a time in his life when that money was the beginning of a new chapter in his life when he was much younger and full of energy. That was when his face and body were handsome and vibrant, and he was married to the love of his life, Millie. They were expecting their first child and the future looked bright. He was unaware of the accident yet to come and the soon to be cursed money awarded to him leading to more tragedy.

6

Life was more than perfect in the eyes of Hector Skeeve. The year was 1954 and Hector had just found out that his young bride of less than a year was pregnant. He had just turned twenty four while Millie was fast approaching her nineteenth birthday right before her delivery due date. There were no two people as in love as they were. Hector Skeeve met and married Millie Herrara within six weeks of meeting her. He was from a small town outside of Nashville, Tennessee and she was from a smaller town called Brownsville in the wild west of Texas. It was there that Hector, who had left home years prior to work on oil rigs off the coast of Texas, that his and Millie's paths crossed. She was a farmgirl who travelled into town to sell home grown vegetables to the local markets. On one of weekly runs to the inner town of Brownsville, she tripped and lost her footing sending the basket of freshly picked corn tumbling to the ground and scattering all about. At a strapping 5'9" with the body of a weight lifter, Hector stopped in his tracks as a piece of corn husk came rolling toward him. He brushed back his light brown hair that hung in his green eyes looking to see where this foreign object of food had come from. Never in his life did he think that the young blonde-haired beauty on her hands and knees scurrying to gather up the ones that had fallen, would be on the receiving end of this misfortunate spill. Nor would or could a girl as beautiful as she, take his breath away. Millie Herrara worked the land of her father's farm. At 5'3", she was not as tall as most girls her age. With ringlets of long blonde hair and eyes the bluest of blue, she was by far the prettiest girl in the southern most tip of Texas.

"Why, howdy there. You look like y'all could use a helping hand if I might say so myself," Hector said as he too bent down

to scoop up some of the fallen husks. "My name is Hector Skeeve and I work on that oil rig a couple of miles out in the ocean. Can't say I ever seen y'all around this part of town before and I've been working in this neck of the woods for almost two years. Now where would a perty girl like you be hiding out?"

Millie, blushing, tried her hardest not to seem too embarrassed over her cluminess, looked over at Hector kneeling within inches of her face, "The name is Millie. Millie Herrara. My father is a Mexican immigrant who married my momma, a Texan herself, and together they purchased some land under my momma's name so that they could farm. Once harvest season is over I come into town and sell our vegetables." Hector stared more astonished by her beauty than anything else. Millie thought he look confused, and that she needed to explain. "And in case you were wondering we plant in April and continue through June. We harvest in October and continue until the end of November. My parents don't ever allow me to hang around this area. I just came into town on a mule with a wagon full of baskets. This was my last run over to the General Store and I guess I was rushing and next thing I knew…….." she stopped herself before she told him just how careless she was that she stumbled. "I appreciate you stopping to help me. These darn husks roll like a bowling ball."

Hector put the last one into her basket and pushed off the ground with one hand and stood up. He then offered his other hand out to Millie, who graciously accepted it. He gently pulled her up onto her feet. Hector then turned to where the basket of corn husks sat on the ground and lifted it up onto his shoulder to balance it all the while saying, "If y'all would be so kind as to point me in the right direction, then I shall be so kind to deliver these for y'all." Millie stared at this new gentlemen in awe.

From the moment their eyes met she knew he was the one. The one who would make her his wife. The one who would father her children. Fortunately, she could not foresee that he would be the one who would, indirectly, be the cause of her very short life.

7

Their courtship lasted a mere month before Hector had asked Mr. Herrara for his daughter's hand in marriage. With her parents' blessings, they were wed two weeks later during the off season of harvesting in January 1954. As luck would have it, Hector was offered a foreman's position just weeks after he took his new bride. The only downside was that the position was in Port Isabel a forty-five minute drive from Millie's parents' farm. Neither her parents nor Hector owned a vehicle which would enable them to drive the distance back and forth to make frequent visits. However, with a promotion and huge pay increase would enable him to afford transportation in no time. So, after a very tearful goodbye with many hugs and long embraces, Hector and Millie set off on their new journey in life. A life that was about to change in an unexpected and unfortunate direction.

8

Together, they found a one-bedroom apartment above a hardware store within walking distance of the piers where Hector boarded ship which would take him out to the oil rigs each week. He would spend two weeks on the rig with one week off. He was responsible for a team of six men. His right-hand man was Ed Suriano, an Italian kid right off the boat. Ed's family settled in the Bronx but he soon followed his uncle to Texas to work on the rigs, where there was the promise of easily made money. His family was very poor and he had made a promise to his mother that he would send whatever money he could back home to help support his seven younger siblings. His father had passed away from a sudden heart attack just weeks after arriving in America. At 6' 1" he was built like a football player and with his physique, he would be a valuable asset on the rig to get the heavy work done. Instantly, he and Ed soon became fast friends, with Hector relying more and more on Ed to get the job done. The only qualm Hector had was that Ed was a chain smoker which was dangerous to the lives of them all upon the oil rig. Often, Hector would tell Ed to put out his cigarette if he felt it was in an area that may be too close for comfort. Jokingly on occasion Ed would pretend to get too close to a flammable zone that would infuriate Hector to the point of no return. He did this more out of lightening up the mood on the somewhat mundane rig that existed day in and day out. A lit cigarette was prohibited anywhere on the rig but three of the six men assigned as Hector's crew were chain smokers. As much as Hector was against this, Hector allowed them to smoke in only designated areas that he deemed as safety zones. Little did he realize that there was no area safe enough to prevent the inevitable.

9

"I feel like the week that you're home goes so fast and the two weeks you're away lasts a lifetime," Millie said in her sweet girlish voice. "I wish you didn't have to be away working all those long hours. I get bored here all by my lonesome. With momma and poppa so far off too, I go stir crazy."

Hector walked over to his wife and gently placed his hand on her belly, "And don't y'all reckon I miss the both of you just as much? Just think, in just six more months you'll be busier than a bee in a honey hive taken care of this here youngin." He rubbed his palm in a circle around her stomach.

"I know, I know. It's just a girl gets lonely for her man. I get all these cravin's and you ain't around to help me out. How am I supposed to run out in the middle of the night to get me some pickles. A girl can never have enough pickles y'all know."

"Is that so? And here I thought my pickle was enough for y'all Millie," Hector replied as they both burst out laughing. "I'll be back before y'all know it. Old man Wilson, who owns the hardware store below us, left us with his phone number just in case you need anything while I'm away. I'm sure he can get y'all a pickle anytime y'all want. Just as long as you don't go asking for the wilted up shriveled up pickle of his." Together, they started laughing as Millie led her husband to the staircase to say her goodbye to the handsome young man that stood before her. "I must say I'm glad y'all work with all those other men. With a face as beautiful as yours I should be the one worrying about where that pickle of yours might be going." She lightly patted his behind as she ushered him out the door to the staircase, "Now y'all get your butt back here fast enough. I miss that pretty face of yours already."

10

It was a quarter to midnight and most of the crew were fast asleep. They had put in a rigorous day on the rig with the task of drilling. At the crack of dawn, the crew set up the rig and started the drilling operation. First, from the starter hole, the team drilled a surface hole down to a pre-set depth, which was somewhere above where they thought the oil trap was located. They then place the drill bit, collar and drill pipe in the hole, attach the Kelly and turntable, and the drilling begins. As the drilling progresses, they circulate mud through the pipe and out of the bit to float the rock cuttings out of the hole. They also add new sections(joints) of drill pipes as the hole gets deeper. They then must remove the drill pipe collar and bit when the pre-set depth is reached. It can be anywhere from a few hundred feet to a couple of thousand feet. Once they reach the pre-set depth, they must run and cement the casing-pipe sections into the hole to prevent it from collapsing in on itself. The effort seems endless and the strain on the men was enduring throughout the day. Hector, himself, had to climb the oil derrick to adjust a steel casing that had come loose from the high winds the day before. Ed assisted him and twice Ed almost lost his footing which would have caused him to plummet fifty feet to the deck. Hector had managed both times to grab hold of him just as Ed's foot had slipped on the oily casing of the steel beams. Now both men leaned against the rail of the platform rehashing the day's events. The winds had calmed down considerably from the previous day with just a slight breeze blowing off the ocean.

"A fine mess we could'a had with you falling off the derrick. Try havin me explain that to our big bosses," Hector said with a harsh tone to his right-hand man.

Ed, with a heavy Italian and Bronx, New York accent, looked his foreman and friend in the eyes and said, "Cutta me some slack. I was just trying to helpa you out. It looked lika you need an extra set of hands upa there. I wasa more afraida for you than anything else. And looka now, all is fine and we fixed those casings justa right."

"I guess y'all are right but you nearly scared the skin off my hide there for a second. Not once but two times I had to grab onto y'all from keep y'all from nosediving. I could really use a nice cold beer right about now. What y'all say?" Hector asked.

"And a nicea shot of tequila to chase it down," Ed said aloud as he reached into his pocket and pulled out a pack of cigarettes. With his other hand, he reached into his dungarees and pulled out a lighter. He lit the cigarette and inhaled. He then proceeded to blow out a perfect ring of white smoke.

Hector was taken back once again by Ed's stupidity. This young kid never seemed to learn his lesson. They couldn't have been more than fifteen feet or less away from slick spots of oil on the floor of the platform.

"Are y'all just crazy or do you have a death wish?," Hector asked as he put his hand out to grab hold of the cigarette that dangled from Ed's lips. "Don't y'all see that oil right over there. God forbid or better still heaven help us or y'all for that matter. Now give me that thing and let's not tempt fate any more than we did already up on the derrick."

Not a moment too soon, Hector took hold of the just started cigarette in the two fingers of his left hand. He moved closer to the rail. He knew the faster he threw the lit butt overboard the safer they would be. Just as he went to fling the cigarette, a stronger than normal breeze caught it in midair and blew it in the opposite direction, straight into the path of the oil residue left along the platform floor.

Hector and Ed watched in horror as the cigarette flew steadily into the spill. The butt ignited the oil so fast that the two men barely had a second to react. The oil caught fire and raced right toward them. A huge flame sparked and an explosion of such great force erupted as the flames shot directly at them with full impact. Hector watched as the flames engulfed Ed's whole body. He then felt a heat so intense that he knew his life was coming to an abrupt end, when suddenly the boards of the platform gave way from the intense heat and collapsed. Both men fell directly into the churning ocean. Hector felt like his face had melted away as he struggled to gain his balance in the water to push himself up to the surface. As he pushed at the water's current his right arm brushed up against an object which to him felt like another human being. With what was the remaining part of his left eye, he saw the twisting object that floated around him. It was the charred remains of his right-hand man, with glazed over eyes that symbolized death.

11

As luck turned out the other five men, positioned at the back of the explosion and one deck below, were uninjured by the mass of destruction to the oil rig. Just as the rig had started to fall apart the five men boarded a lifeboat and dropped it into the water. Not knowing where or what procedure to follow next, they watched as the flames rose up into the sky lighting the surrounding area as if it were daytime. As they waited for help to arrive by staying clear of the rig, one of the men pointed to *a floating object yards away from them. They slowly paddled their way over and upon closer inspection, discovered it was their foreman, half burned but still alive. They delicately pulled him into the lifeboat and within the hour the coast guard had arrived and ushered them all to safety. It wasn't for another two days that Ed's barely recognizable body had washed up onto the shore.*

12

Hector had been in the burn trauma unit of the hospital for eight weeks undergoing surgery upon surgery to reconstruct his severely burned face. Plastic surgeons were non-existent in the mid-fifties in a small coastal hospital. The doctors did the best they could but the damage to his face was beyond repair. Hector's nose was destroyed with just nostrils where his nose once was. They removed skin from his inner thighs to reconstruct his lips. A deep color purple covered the whole right side of his face and his right eye drooped from below his missing eyebrow. The first time he saw himself in the mirror he saw a hideous monster staring back. At first, even Millie who used to joke how handsome he was found it hard to look directly at him. While all these procedures were taking place, Southern Crude Oil Purchasing Company sent their representatives and top lawyers to settle a claim for the hardship he now suffered. Recalling the events that took place and realizing that if he did tell them the actual truth, Hector fabricated a whole different tale as to what had happened. Knowing that Ed would never be around to tell what did indeed take place and at whose hands the actual explosion occurred, Hector blamed the cigarette that Ed lit up that fateful night. He said that he warned Ed to put it out and Ed refused. The next thing he knew flames were engulfing the both of them. The rest was a blur. The lawyers had questioned the other five survivors who testified to the fact that Ed was a very heavy smoker. The Oil company had compensated the other five men accordingly and didn't leave any money for the loss of Ed's life. Although his mother had begged the lawyers that he was her only source of income to support her and her children, they refused any monetary payout. The high-end lawyers told her she was very lucky they didn't go after her for the punitive damages that were being paid out. Hector Skeeve, however, was awarded a hefty sum for being disabled and unable to work for their company in the future. Southern Crude Oil settled with him for a whopping 2.1 million dollars. A sum of that proportion was unheard of back in those days, but one look at the face of Hector Skeeve and any settlement would never be enough. Hector and Millie fast agreed upon the amount and an account had been set up in their names with the total deposit in place the week before he was discharged from the hospital. Hector Skeeve signed all the paperwork releasing the company from any future claims against them. He vowed to never tell the truth to anyone of what actually took place on the horrible night. He swore to himself that he would even lie to his wife if she ever asked. Never in his marriage would he ever think that possible. Ed was made to be the sole person responsible for the loss of many millions of dollars when all was said and done. Hector had to live with that lie. That lie that would eventually come back to haunt him for all the days of his life.

13

It was a colder than normal day in November less than two weeks before Millie's due date. She, herself, had just turned nineteen. They had traveled back home to spend her birthday with her parents on their farm. The very first purchase they made with their huge settlement was a brand new 1954 Ford Customline Country Sedan. It took them over an hour to reach Millie's old home. Upon seeing Hector for the first time since the accident, Millie's parents were unable to make eye contact when they spoke to him. They were unable to previously visit due to lack of transportation. Hector was now used to the pitiful stares from strangers but he would never be able to get used to loving family members turning away in disgust from him. Sensing the uneasiness he experienced, he feigned a sudden illness coming on and left Millie the remaining days to be alone with her parents.

14

Hector had just gotten out of bed and wandered into the kitchen to start a pot of coffee for himself. He had been home alone for four days now and he was to pick Millie up on Sunday afternoon. He wasn't looking forward to seeing Millie's parents again and they were probably feeling the same way about him. Millie had made a point to call him twice a day to check up on him. The conversation was light and more about the soon to be delivered child. She told him how much she missed him and he in reply said the same. Millie never mentioned her parents and he knew it was a subject too tender for her to broach. Having a sudden urge to pee, Hector backtracked to the bathroom to relieve himself. He dared not look in the bathroom mirror. The image that stared back at him in all actuality frightened him. While he was in the bathroom, he thought he heard what was a light knocking upon his front door. They never got visitors. At least not since the accident and the way he now looked. People steered clear of him. Most of the time he would hear footsteps coming up the stairs of the flat above the hardware store but this time he heard nothing. Just a light tapping. Hector walked over to the door and opened it just enough to see who had been knocking. On the other side of the door was a stout woman who appeared to be in her early forties at most. She had her hair, which appeared to be all gray pulled back and up under a woolen hat. A dark scarf hung around her neck and she wore a tattered coat that had seen many years of use. There was no one else with her.

Hector opened the door a little wider and asked, "How may I help y'all? Do I know you somehow?"

The woman who now had a much clearer look at his face took a step back and answered, "Gooda Lord. I don't know if the Lord dida right by sparing you. If my Eddie would have looked likea that, I don't know howa his brothas and sistas would be able to deal with him."

Upon hearing the name Eddie, Hector now knew who this short stout woman was. The heavy Italian accent also confirmed his assumption. Ed's mother. Last he knew she lived all the way up north on the east coast in a place called the Bronx. "Pardon me maam, but aren't y'all Ed's mom?"

"Yes thata be mea. I'm Susanna. Susanna Suriano. I tooka my first plane ride and a cab from the airport all the way ova herea to see youa in person. I tried callin you buta no one picked

up the phone the last few times over the course of a few monthas. My neighbors all chipped ina to buy me a rounda trip airlina ticket to comea see youa in person. They evena gavea mea money to get a caba back and fortha to your addressa here. I had to calla many people to get herea where you liveda. I hearda from thosea big timea lawyers thata you were given so so mucha money. Nowa I see why'all. Poor poor thinga. How doa ou go about a your daily lifea?"

Hector was astonished to hear her asking him how he lived his life in his disfigured state. And to say poor, poor thing. Pity was very evident all over her facial expressions. He let her continue to speak.

"I a get right to the pointa. I needa money. Lots of money for my'all kids and mea. My deara Eddie, rest his soula, was my'all only means of incomea. New Yorka state givesa me a little money but notta anuff to geta by. You havea lots of money'all I hearda. Morea than any one persona can spenda in a lifetime. Please givea me somea. I needa your helpa. Eddie woulda wanta this froma you." Hector listened the whole while and let the words sink in. This woman had the audacity to gaze with pitiful stares and at the same time plead for money. Not just a small sum but if he heard her correctly lots of money. Having now heard enough of her begging, Hector looked her squarely in the eyes saying in the most callous way, "Why should I give y'all any of MY money. I earned in rightfully so. I mean look at my face. And by the look on your face I see that you have done that in a very sorrowful way. I aint giving y'all or any of y'all kind a stitch of my money. If it weren't for your careless son to begin with......."

Susanna, taken back by his harsh rudeness, with tears now forming in her eyes pleaded, "Buta we needa money and

*youa have it all. My Eddie no be the careless onea. Something
tellsa me youa are hiding something, I sensa it from the whole
presence of youra being. The Good Lord and my Jesus area tellin
me thisa. Whata really happened thata night Mister Skeevea?
Nowa is your chance to redeema youselfa with the Father, Sona
and Holy Spirit."*

Hector was infuriated at this short dumpy woman who
questioned his integrity and wanted to know the truth of what
really happened the night of the oil rig explosion. How she
sensed he was lying was unimaginably impossible but Hector
sensed she really did see right through him. Perhaps she was
some sort of psychic. Also, in a haste to climb the steps, Susanna
had forgotten to pull the front door on the side of the hardware
store shut and the wind had suddenly picked up. Suddenly,
Hector started to perspire even though the breeze coming up the
stairs was colder than normal for this time of year. A flashback
of that night on the platform of the rig passed before his eyes.
The same sort of breeze caught the cigarette that he, Hector
Skeeve, tossed into the air that distant night months ago. As
the sweat started to drip from his forehead down his face,
Susanna continued to rant and rave about Hector writing
her a check before she left. Hector tuned her out as he slowly
started to close the door in her face never to open it again until
she was gone. Susanna tried in vain to push it in to no avail.
Knowing that she was getting nowhere, she slid down along
the door sobbing uncontrollably with one last hope that this
deformed man would rescue her from despair. She sat there
for a good hour or more crying and cursing in Italian. When
she regained her composure, she bent over to speak into the
key hole of the door. *"I knowa youa can heara me, Hector
Skeevea. Until youa do righta to people nothing gooda will*

ever comea your way. May the money you havea be cursed for all of youra future generations. And the blood be washed upon youra handsa. The devil did righta by the looka youra facea." Susanna reached for the crucifix she had hidden under her blouse. She kissed Jesus on the cross silently asking for his forgiveness and placed the cross back near her heart. She then in the next moment with her pinkie and index finger pointed straight at the door. Trying to be silent and under her breath, she chanted an old ritual that her great grandmother has passed down many generations before. Susanna placed what is known as the Malocchio (pronounced Ma loi key) curse upon Hector. According to Italian superstition, the malocchio then manifests itself in some sort of misfortune onto the cursed person. Other Italians also refer to it as The Evil Eye. In either case the person is wished nothing but misfortune and bad luck. Half smiling to herself, that Hector would soon see his world start to crumble, and now in complete control of her emotions, Susanna stood up straight and started down the staircase. Knowing that she would never get a dime out of the hideous young man, and she never looked back.

15

The next few days Hector did nothing but lay around and sulk. He hadn't felt right since Ed's mother had paid him a visit insisting he give her money. The audacity of her to think he should just write her a check. Ed was gone and probably better off that he didn't survive to look like he did. Then as he listened on the other side of his door, Hector swore the old lady was mumbling some sort of prayer or for better words witchcraft from what he was picking up. As soon as he heard her footsteps descending the stairs he stopped sweating. In place came shivers and the chills causing him to rush into the living room to grab a blanket off the couch. For the next two days, he barely moved since every muscle ached in his body. He didn't even bother picking up after himself, leaving the house an utter mess. Now, he patiently counted the remaining days before he picked up Millie. On top of everything else, their apartment was suffocating to him when he was alone. Once the baby came, Hector planned on buying a house somewhere far away from this crappy little town. He planned on heading off to a distant place in another state to start a new life in a new home. Since Millie was an only child, he would extend the invitation for her parents to move with them. They would have to sell their farm. If they did venture along, he hoped they would be able to look him in the face without repulsion. Being able to face their son-in-law even as gruesome as he appeared, would mean they could all live happily ever after. This thought would be a fairytale that would never actually take place.

16

Waking up at the crack of dawn, Hector, although still not feeling a hundred percent, started to get ready to pick up the love of his life. He made the drive to the Herrara farm. As he drove up the dirt road, he spotted Millie waiting outside on the porch. Millie looked like she was ready to burst carrying their child as she made her way down the steps and over to the car. She leaned into the passenger window which Hector had already rolled down. Hector asked where her parents were to say hello and goodbye. Looking uncomfortable, she made up an excuse that both her parents were under the weather and said to pass along their greetings. Millie then asked Hector to grab her suitcase at the bottom of the steps to load in the trunk. Hector scrambled out of the car, rushed over to Millie and tenderly hugged and kissed her. He cherished her in every way possible. Never did she look at him in a disgusted way. She loved him wholeheartedly and he felt it just being near her. As he lifted the suitcase, he had an uneasy feeling that this piece of baggage was too heavy for her to carry down the steps. Someone else had carried it down for her. Someone who would never let his daughter carry such a heavy load. Millie's father. That is what a father would do. The hard-working man Hector was proud to have as his father-in-law until just now. The man who wasn't even man enough to face him anymore.

17

As soon as they arrived home, Millie noticed the apartment was a complete and utter mess. It looked as if someone threw a party with way too many guests. Everything was askew. Without even taking off her coat she started picking up after what Hector had strewn about. Dirty dishes were left on the counter and not even placed in the sink. It looked like he just left his clothes wherever he took them off, as if he just stepped out of them and walked away. Millie was furious and didn't know where to begin. Hector immediately sensed her temper starting to flare just by the glances she gave in his direction and tried to make up an excuse to soften the blows he knew were about to come, "I told y'all that I wasn't myself those last few days and it took all I had to just to get through the day. I shoulda cleaned up a bit. I'm sorry my sweet pea." Hector walked over and placed his arm gently around her neck from behind and kissed the back of her head.

Slightly annoyed, Millie brushed his arm off her neck, "Don't ya sweet pea me. Honestly Hector. This place looks like a tornado hit it. I don't need this right now. I should be sitting down with my feet up. Remember what Doctor Shore said. I can go into labor at any time now. Besides all that, Doctor Shore was also monitoring my blood pressure the last few visits. It spiked the last few times he checked and an elevated blood pressure isn't good. So either way I can deliver two weeks before or two weeks after. And right now I can feel my blood pressure boiling." The sweat was dripping off the ends of her blonde locks as she wiped them away. She continued bending over to scoop up plates and utensils.

Hector stood there with both his arms at his sides. He knew that it had to do with Ed's momma. Ever since she left nothing had felt right. He felt like everything was a strain. The simplest chore was a challenge. It took Hector enormous effort to just get out of bed. He hadn't yet told Millie of his encounter with Mrs. Suriano. Deep down he knew if he told her the conversation that transpired, Millie would be even more upset at how he handled the whole thing. If Millie was present, she would have reasoned with him and made him give the woman some money. Maybe not as much as the old woman thought she deserved but something. Hector wanted it all and felt he deserved it. Even if the accident was his fault, he had to live out the rest of his life disfigured. Ed was gone and there was no bringing him back. In due time, he knew he would tell Millie about the encounter, but right now in the state she was in that was just going to add fuel to the fire. He didn't believe in keeping secrets from her. He would wait until he felt she was much more calm. Now, as he watched his young wife moving around like a lightning bolt, he became even more guilt ridden, "Sit, please sit. Let me do this. You need to relax like y'all said. Ain't gonna help y'all by sweatin so bad as y'all are now. Let me at least get that coat of yours off." Hector raised his arms and reached over again but this time to remove her heavy woolen winter coat.

Millie was so upset at this point that she moved out of his way, "Please Hector, I really didn't need to clean up after you. Its gonna take me a full day or two to get this place back in some sort of......I can't even think of a word to...... oh right, a semblance of what the apartment used to look like. Millie started to bend over to pick up a coffee mug when she doubled over in pain crying out. Hector ran up to her and put his arms on both her sides to lift her up.

"Oh God, Hector. Somethin ain't right." Again, she cried out, "The baby. The baby is coming. I just know it. Oh.... God.............Here.....it comes....again." Millie let Hector raise her up until she was standing. "Y'all better just get me to the stairs, and to the hospital."

Panicked and out of breath himself Hector said, "Let me call Doctor Shore's office. I'll let Basha know that we're headin over now and have him meet us at the hospital." And before he even made it over to the phone on the kitchen wall, he felt something wet beneath his feet. When he looked down, both his shoes were now in a puddle of water.

He looked over at Millie who was now red-faced in agony and watched as she mouthed the words, "Good God Hector, my water just broke."

18

Practically carrying her down the stairs in both his arms, Hector rushed over to the car and placed her down. He opened the passenger door and gently ushered her in. Once he tucked her into the seat, he ran around to the driver side, jumped in and sped off. Dolly Vinsant Memorial Hospital in San Benito was a thirty-five minute ride away. He knew a faster route than the main highway that wasn't heavily used by other vehicles and opted to go that way. While trying to focus on the road and look over at his wife who had now started to pant, it took Hector complete control not to go off the road. Twice, Millie let out life piercing screams, rattling Hectors nerves. He knew it was just a matter of time before the baby would need to come out. At the maximum speed the car would allow, they were half way there when suddenly Hector felt the whole car pull to the right. He braced his hands on the wheel as the car began to rattle on the front passenger side.

"Mother of mercy. Not now. Please not now," he pleaded out loud to his wife's deafening cries. It took all he had not to veer off the road with the pull from the flat tire. About a half mile back a pick-up truck coming down the opposite side of the two-laned road, swerved to avoid hitting a stray dog, and crossed over the center line. Hector saw this off in the distance and had ample time to move closer to the shoulder. It was while driving on the shoulder that the tire ran over a nail or sharp object causing the tire to instantly deflate.

Hector slowed the car down since they had been riding on the rim for a good amount of time. Millie who had been taking slow deep breaths opened her eyes and upon seeing the car now at a dead stop began sobbing, "Oh God no, please noooo......

Tell me this isn't happening." A contraction took hold of her again as her back raised up off the seat as she cried out, "Not now. Please Lord. Not......now!" Hector didn't know what to do. Panic overwhelmed him and he jumped out of the car.

"Stay put Millie. I'll get this here tire changed in no time flat."

There was a pause in her contraction and the while he could hear her muttering, "Why us? Why now? What did we do to deserve this? Aren't we good enough Christians?" When suddenly another contraction twice the intensity. "Oh..... God....Hector. The baby.....is COMING." Millie had her knees pushed tightly together trying to keep the baby from making its way down the canal.

Hector ran in circles. First to the trunk and then to the passenger side to check on his wife. Back and forth like a lost puppy. Not knowing what else to do, he ran into the middle of the road to flag down the next car that passed in either direction. There was no time to change the flat. Millie needed medical care now. Since this road wasn't a highly used one, he stood waving his arms frantically back and forth to no avail all the while hearing Millie continue to question how this was happening to them.

Then from the other direction Hector spotted a car heading towards them. He ran across the road and crossed the center line knowing he would have to stop the car even if it meant throwing himself in front of it. The car had no choice but to slow down, and the woman behind the wheel looked totally frightened by this crazy man throwing his arms in the air and jumping up and down in the middle of the road.

"Help us, PLEASE help us! My wife is in labor and we just got a flat. I need to get her to the hospital NOW!"

The lady looked over at the car on the shoulder and saw a young woman in the passenger seat. From this distance it looked as if the young woman was in severe pain. As it turned out, the woman had just finished her shift as a nurse at Dolly Vinsant Hospital and was on her way home. She drove across the lanes and parked her car in front of theirs. Hector ran over to her thanking her the whole time.

"We need to get her to the hospital. PLEASE!"

Wearing her nurses uniform, the woman in her early thirties with dark hair pulled back in a ponytail, knew this situation was critical. She went over to the door and opened it softly saying, "Sweetie, my name's Elyse. Elyse Kinch and I'm a nurse. Can y'all hear me? Y'all need to answer me this simple question. Okay?"

Millie looked over at this angel sent from heaven with eyes the color of the sky and answered her, "Yes, I hear y'all." The contractions had eased for the moment. "My baby is coming. Please help us." Her eyes flitted as she was trying to explain further. "Every minute or so they come......or no...sweet Jesus....."

Another contraction took hold of Millie again as Elyse yelled over to Hector that they weren't going anywhere. The baby was being delivered now. Elyse told him to gather any type of cloth he could. Having just gotten home that day, Hector hadn't taken Millie's suitcase from the trunk yet. He ran to the back and pulled the suitcase out, dropping it on the concrete road. Not another car passed as he was pulling out various garments from the luggage. He cursed himself for not taking the main highway at this point. Other cars could have stopped to assist. Hector ran with a blouse or two to hand over to Elyse. And as he gave them to her, he was more than grateful that at least she was a trained professional.

Elyse barked out orders to Hector and he followed them. Elyse, not until now, noticed Hector's face. She surmised he was badly burned in a fire, having seen other patients in the hospital with similar scars in the burn unit. They had since laid Millie across the whole front seat with her knees bent. She instructed Hector to get as many clothes as he could find lined up under Millie to prop her up. He did as he was told. Elyse knelt half on the seat and half out the door, all the while guiding Millie through childbirth. Hector wiped his wife's brow and tried to soothe her as she screamed out with each push. It was only after three short pushes that a head full of dark hair first entered the world. Elyse kept praising the job this young woman was doing and reached in to help guide the baby out. Once the bay was fully out she took the pliers that she asked Hector to grab out of the tool box he kept in his trunk and cut the umbilical cord separating the mother from her child. She did what all nurses were trained to do in school and flipped the baby upside down and gave it a soft whack on its behind. No sooner did Elyse take her hand away from the newborn infant, the boy started to wail. Hector watched in total awe as she wrapped their new bundle of joy in another blouse he pulled from Millie's suitcase.

Amazed and proud of the job of delivering her first baby by herself and never imagining she could have done so, she gently placed the baby onto Millie's chest. "I reckon I'll be tellin this story for the rest of my nursing days. Y'all are the proud new parents of what looks like to me a healthy baby boy. I'd say once y'all are feeling a bit better we load y'all in my car and get you over to the hospital right away. Y'all can get the car fixed later."

Hector watched as his wife held onto their new son with all her might. He knew this little boy would get the most love he could from his momma. He took hold of her one hand and squeezed it lightly whispering in her ear, "Y'all are gonna be the bestest momma there is. Y'all know that. Sorry for this little mishap along the way, but I reckon' like Nurse Elyse said. We will all have some heck of a story to tell this youngin' when he gets older."

Millie who still looked paler than normal just stared into her son's eyes. She was drenched in sweat and still shaking somewhat. I think we should name him Nathaniel. I read it means the Gift of God."

"I like that! Nathaniel it is! He is our Gift of God. And just the idea of how he came to be out here on this darn old road! The name is perfect considering the circumstances of his birth."

Elyse was not saying much as she let these new parents take in the new child. She did want to clean up Millie and get her to the hospital right away. She was certain they would need to do certain procedures she wasn't capable of out here in the middle of nowhere. "I say we get y'all cleaned up and on our way to the hospital and if I must say so myself, I too, like that choice of name. Not having any children of my own, I guess any child would be a gift from God."

Hector thanked her once and twice again. He couldn't believe how fortunate it was that of all people, a nurse came to their rescue. He edged his way out of the car so Elyse could help get Millie and the baby get ready for their short journey to the hospital.

Millie had just handed Nathaniel over to Elyse and felt the need to also thank this angel sent from heaven, "Thank you Elyse! Honestly, we can't thank y'all enough. I promise we will make it up to y'all. Ain't that right Hector. Give her some of that settlement that we couldn't spend in two lifetimes. Once we get this little guy home, I'll see to it that you are well taken *care……." Millie stopped speaking as her whole body started to convulse. From her head to her toes she went into some type of a seizure. One after the other wracked her body for a full ten minutes. Elyse once again started to shout out orders to Hector after she handed over his son to him. She was trying to hold down Millie's body as it kept rising and falling in uncontrollable spasms, Millie was now foaming from the mouth.*

"Listen sweetie, hang on for me. Okay? Y'all got a new baby son here to raise. Nathaniel, the gift from God needs his momma. You hear me. He NEEDS his MOMMA!" Having been a nurse for the past ten years Elyse knew exactly what was happening to this poor young girl. It was called eclampsia, causing very high blood pressure, leading to seizures and without proper medical attention it could be fatal. Tears had started to well in her eyes as Elyse took hold of Millie's hand to squeeze it as she passed on from this life. It was futile to try and deny the fact that she would soon be gone. In one final extreme spasm, her thrashing body shook violently one last time.

Millie knew something wasn't right as soon as she passed little Nathaniel over to Elyse. She felt her whole inner being fighting to stay alive. As soon as the thrashing began, Millie knew this was the beginning of the end. As she rose up and down in seizures, she saw her young life pass before her eyes. She knew she would never see her loving parents again nor feel the tender embrace of her ever-loving husband. The most painful part of all was never being there to raise her son Nathaniel. A gift from God. A God that was waiting with open arms for her to enter his kingdom. Although she wasn't afraid to meet her maker, she was terrified of leaving her newborn son. As Millie took her last breath of life before giving in to death, a single tear rolled down her cheek for the son she would never see grow up.

Hector was frozen in place holding his newborn son. At first, he thought with the nurse present, all would be okay. But then after a few minutes of watching the love of his life's body continually rise and fall, a dread like no other took over his inner being. It was at the precise second that Millie closed her eyes for all of eternity, that Hector knew his life would never ever be the same. In a last-ditch effort to say anything at all to his dying wife, all that managed to escape his lips was, "NOOOOOOOO!"

19

Shortly after her death, Millie was buried in the local cemetery a half mile out of town. Having known Millie all her life, most of the townspeople came to her funeral on a crisp late November day. The only memories Hector recalled of the services were blurry images of people offering their condolences, as even then in the darkest of times, they were unable to look at him as they did so. The first few weeks passed by in a blur as each day went into the next. Hanna Herrara, Millie's mother, spent the first month at Hector's apartment caring for her deceased daughter's child, her grandchild Nathaniel. Hanna, and her husband Miguel, were distraught over the loss of their only child and it appeared to have aged them overnight. Both their faces were withdrawn, not only from the years of hard labor on the farm, but from the grief they each had to endure so suddenly. The only consolation they had was that they were able to spend her last week with her at their farm, laughing and talking about the future of Millie and her unborn child. Millie would tease them saying they were much too young to be a granny and poppa. This would cause them to all burst out laughing. Hanna and Miguel had to bury their heartbreak for now and mourn in due time. They realized that their son-in-law wouldn't be able to deal with his own grief upon losing his wife, and on top of that, raising his infant son would be too much for him to handle. Decisions had to be made. With no uncertainty, Hanna insisted on staying with Hector and Nathaniel until the time was right to go back to her husband at their farm. As painful as Hector's appearance was for her to look upon, her grandson was her main concern. Hanna would have to deal with his disfigurement the best she could. Her whole time there, it was a very uncomfortable situation all around. To Hector it felt like whenever he entered a room of the apartment, Hanna would take the baby as soon as he came near and go to another. This became a normal routine for them. Hanna would rise, as she was used to on their farm, at the crack of dawn, and care for the baby until the sunset when she would go to sleep with her grandson by nightfall. Hector mulled around the apartment all day trying to keep his mind from snapping and throwing him into the pit of despair upon losing Millie. He knew his and his son's life would never be the same. He was a prisoner not only in his apartment but in this whole town as well. Every single person knew of the accident and how his deformed face came to be. He no longer wandered around the streets of Port Isabel either. Hector felt suffocated. If he didn't break free of this town, he would burst. But deep down, he was afraid of what the future for him and Nathaniel might hold anywhere beyond here. With a deep realization, he knew this is where he would remain all the days of his life. What he didn't realize was that his in-laws had a different plan of their own.

20

The years passed, but the heartbreak remained for all except little Nathaniel. For the past four years of Nathaniel's life, Hector parented his child to the best of his ability. He would visit Millie's parents every couple of weeks on a Sunday. In the beginning, he would try and stay for most of an afternoon. Hanna and Miquel adored their grandson but found it very hard to make any conversation with their son-in-law. Making eye contact was still extremely difficult for them to do. The air was tinged with awkwardness. Soon, the visits became less and less frequent, and with each one, the Herrara's became less cordial to Hector. They pretended he wasn't there and doted only on Nathaniel. Then on a late Sunday afternoon while Hector sat out of the front porch hearing his son giggle with his granny and poppa, Hanna came through the screen door with a tray on which two glasses of iced tea were standing. Again, while staring off at her cornstalks and never making eye contact, she placed a glass of iced tea on the small table between the rocking chairs. Hanna took the other seat and lifted her own glass taking a sip and said in the kindest voice possible, "Miguel and I have been giving this a lot of thought. Before y'all know it, Nathaniel will be getting ready for school. A darlin' little boy like him will need the guidance of people who can raise him the right way. He needs to go to Church every Sunday and to visit his momma's grave. Ya'll know I asked him if he had ever seen his momma and where she sleeps and he had no idea. He looked at me here like I had two heads." Hanna caught herself as soon as she made reference to the two heads. "No disrespect to ya'll Hector about the two heads. I meant that……."

Hector didn't take any offense to what she said but he was very curious as to where this conversation was leading, "I do right by my boy. No need to take him to a Church. Why go to see a God that took my Millie away."

Having an edge to her voice she continued, "She was OUR Millie too. Don't ya'll think we miss her just as much. She was all we had here. I thank the good Lord each and every day for sparing this beautiful little angel on that God forsaken road y'all chose to……" Hanna stopped talking as she knew she said too much.

"For the love of God, please tell me y'all aren't blaming me for what happened. For the route I took to get my Millie the fastest way to the hospital. Y'all should be ashamed of yaself if that's the case. And from the sound of it and what y'all might be getting at, my son and I are just getting along fine."

Hanna knew she had to tread more carefully to get her point across, "Hector," she took his hand from across the small table where the two glasses stood, and still not making eye contact continued, "It's just that Nathaniel needs to go to school next year and the school is only a quarter of a mile from our farm. I can walk him to and from school each day. He'll make lots of friends and be able to have friends come over to play after school and…….." Once again her words spun in a direction that would not bode well with Hector.

"And what, Hanna, what? The other kids won't have to look at this face of mine." His voice began to rise as Miguel came out the front door with Nathaniel in his arms. "I know I'm hideous to look at. Y'all remind me of that each and every God forsaken time I visit y'all. But to want me to just give y'all my little boy to raise so that he doesn't have other kids make fun of him just ain't right. And y'all know what else ain't right. I'll

tell y'all. That y'all call yaselfs God's people. Would God himself look down on me. Apparently so he does. I suffer every darn day just getting through it. I see the stares and looks of disdain from other people and I live with it. I have NO choice! These are the cards I was dealt for surviving that day so many years ago." *Hector walked over to Miguel, who stood there speechless, and grabbed his son out of his poppa's arms. Nathaniel started to cry.* *"But I will tell y'all one thing for sure. I do have a choice when it comes to this boy of mine. And come hell or high water, NO ONE, not even y'all, will take him away from me. I may have lost my Millie and y'all may always blame me for that, but by the grace of this dear good God, if there is one, ain't anybody ever takin this boy away from me."* *Hector marched down the porch steps and left Hanna and Miguel staring directly at him with wide eyes and their mouths agape.*

21

The very next day Hector walked into the Five & Ten and purchased an oversized style duffel bag. With Nathaniel in tow he marched into the First National Bank and asked for the manager. He requested that his account be closed and that he wanted the remaining balance of his settlement wrapped in stacks of hundreds. The bank manager, a tall lean man named Mitchell Sommer, had said that a large amount of currency such as his would require a few days to gather and complete the transaction. Mr. Sommer asked that since the work week had only begun would Mr. Skeeve be so kind as to give them until Thursday to fulfill his request. Hector agreed and set off to do what he thought he must do next.

22

At exactly nine o'clock on Thursday morning Hector, with Nathaniel beside him, were first in line at the doors of First National Bank. He had parked his car up the block and out of view as to not raise any questions. He was immediately greeted by Mitchell Sommer, who had thanked him for his patience this past few days while his request was put through. Mr. Sommer asked Hector to take a seat over by his desk while he went to get the security guard. Together, Mr. Sommer and the bank security guard walked over. The security guard was built like a big black bear. No one in their right mind would mess with him for fear of retaliation. In his one hand he easily carried the duffle bag that Hector had purchased the other day and had left for them to fill with his requested cash. Among handshakes and goodbyes, Mr. Sommer thanked Mr. Skeeve for the years of business they shared together and if there was ever a future need to feel free to come back. The loss of that kind of money from their bank was a big hit in any sense. Hector took hold of the duffle bag that was placed at his feet. It was much heavier than he imagined and with all his strength took hold of it and with his other free hand grabbed onto Nathaniel's hand leaving the bank never to return again.

23

That same day Hector drove straight out of Port Isabel and headed northeast to drive up Interstate 95 which was being constructed all along the east coast since the mid-fifties. Hector *knew where he intended to wind up and with nothing but free time on his hands and the love of this little boy next to him, he drove on.*

24

Sixteen days later, having made this whole experience a road trip, Hector stopped in a town called West Dover in Vermont. There was a tiny real estate office in the next town over, where he first stopped. A sweet petite real estate woman who at first was taken back by his appearance slowly adjusted her reaction on this young man who stood before her with a cute young boy in tow. The little boy had curly light brown hair and his eyes sparkled green with visions of a future still unclear. Cheryl Mills, the real estate agent asked Hector what he had in mind as far as property and home, listened intently and told him she had just the place according to his wants and needs. It was a tiny two-bedroom log cabin situated on 650 acres of land not too far from Mount Snow, a ski resort that opened back in 1954. As that had been the same year Hector met Millie, without any other questions, he told her he would take it. Never in all her years of real estate had Cheryl Mills made such a quick sale, nevermind the fact that the whole transaction was paid in cash! With the help of the owner of the real estate agency the whole deal took less than six hours after he arrived at their door, making Hector the proud new owner of his own cabin and hundreds of acres of land.

25

As soon as he was settled in, Hector did the right thing by registering his only son Nathaniel to start kindergarten that fall. Since his birthday wasn't until late November, he would be younger than most other kids his age in school. Nathaniel adjusted well to their new life and soon stopped asking if they would ever go see his granny and poppa again. Hector knew that leaving the way he did was the best for all involved and often wondered just how heartbroken Hanna and Miguel were. To get past his guilt of deserting the only other family Nathaniel would ever have, once again, he blamed them for the conversation they had the last day he saw them. It made it easier to push the blame on them instead of him. The years slowly passed and Nathaniel continued to grow, as Hector lived off his settlement. Once again Hector was a prisoner in his own home as he rarely left the cabin.

26

Nathaniel never brought any friends home and often pleaded with his father to let him go their houses instead. Hector knew the reason but never questioned his son. The years continued to breeze by and Nathaniel was now taller than his father. He stood a tall 6' 2" and his once boyish body was now nicely built, and he became an avid skier at the nearby mountain. Every weekend Nathaniel would plead with his father to let him spend the weekend at a friend's house so they could get up early and be the first on the chair lifts at Mount Snow. When *he became a sophomore, Nathaniel joined the ski patrol at the mountain, enabling him to earn his own money. Hector, although more wealthy than imaginable, was still frugal when it came to Nathaniel. It wasn't until 1972 when Nathaniel was a senior in high school soon to graduate in the spring that Hector had a huge surprise for him. Nathaniel had decided to go to college locally at Marlboro College a short twenty-minute drive away. He wanted to study medicine with the hopes of one day becoming a doctor. The day of his eighteenth birthday, Hector drove his son in their 1970 Jeep Wrangler he had recently purchased after trading in his first car from long ago. A little less than a mile away from their two-bedroom log cabin, Hector stopped the jeep in a clearing they came upon a newly built log cabin. Hector handed over a set of keys that looked as new as the cabin before them.*

Nathaniel took hold of the keys, staring through the front windshield, gazing at this newly built cabin.

"Happy birthday boy! You are eighteen now. Can't have y'all living in that tiny little place of ours when you're going off to college next year. Figured a man needs his own place so I went and had this three-bedroom log cabin built just for y'all. This way y'all have your own place just up the road from y'all old man. You can have your friends stay whenever y'all want. After all, I know you didn't want to invite friends back to the old place." Hector looked away as he finished that last sentence.

Nathaniel was in shock seeing what his father had done. Although they never talked about the reason why Nathaniel never brought other kids home, it was something they both knew. Nathaniel took hold of his father's hand, and with all the love a son could have for his Dad, simply said, "Thanks Dad! I love you more than you could ever know. I'm sorry if I…….."

Hector reached over and put a finger to his son's lips stopping him from finishing his sentence and simply said, "Hush up my son. Now get on out of this car and check out.......What do y'all kids say now.......this here DIGS!"

27

As life itself moved along, the next four years flew by. Nathaniel went off to college each semester and earned a place on the Dean's list, as Hector became more and more of a recluse. Hector paid the tuition in full each semester so that his son would have a debt free college education. He also set aside money for medical school as Nathaniel told him of his interest in becoming a doctor. Their time together was infrequent leaving Hector to fend for himself. Hector despised doing errands in town. It was on one such outing, that Hector met an older woman in town, as he shopped in the local grocery store to pick up a few things, painfully aware of the pitiful stares coming his way. She felt bad for him and sensing that she could make his life easier, said because she lived close by, she could pick up what few items he might need weekly. To Hector this was a blessing in disguise. Even though Nathaniel commuted back and forth from West Dover to Marlboro college, living in the cabin Hector had built for him, their time together was limited, as Nathaniel had a very busy schedule. Nathaniel still made time for his father as often as he could, but since deciding that he wanted to study to be a doctor, the college workload took up most of his time. Nathaniel had wanted to be a OBGYN and one day hopefully open his own practice. He also met a girl named Jenna Pepe who was going to the same college to become a nurse. Unbeknownst to Hector, the two had, as they now said in the mid-seventies been 'shacking up' at Nathaniel's cabin the last few months. Nathaniel had never mentioned his father's appearance to this girl he had fallen in love with. All in due time Nathaniel thought. He would know when the time was right to finally introduce them. What Nathaniel was unaware of, was there never would be the right time.

28

Hector woke up earlier than normal. He stretched and for the first time in weeks felt better than he had in quite some time. Usually, each morning upon waking, his muscles ached and he had to work out the kinks throughout his body before he got out of bed. Hector got up and quickly took a shower and dressed. He wanted to see his son. Although they lived not too far from one another, his son's hectic schedule kept them apart. Nathaniel did call him on a regular basis to check in and say hello. But he hadn't seen him for way longer than he was used to. It was Sunday and Hector took a chance that Nathaniel may be sleeping in. He never really just showed up without a phone call first, but in this case a quick visit couldn't really do them any harm.

29

Jenna Pepe, at a small 5'1", was strikingly beautiful. Her long dark hair reached down her back and almost touched the cheeks of her behind. Often guys were mesmerized by her eyes and would tell her that she could probably hypnotize them just by staring into the dark blue of them. More often than not, she had her choice of the guys by the dozens, but it was the charm of Nathaniel that had won her affection. The minute her hypnotizing eyes met his, it was love at first sight. Jenna always found it odd how people would say they knew right off the bat and from that instant, they found their soulmate. Upon her first gaze into Nathaniel's baby blues, she was smitten. They became a couple right away, and before she knew it she had moved in with him. Her love for him grew more and more intense as each day lead to the next and she was certain that once they had finished their degrees, she would be Mrs. Jenna Skeeve. While those happy thoughts dancing around gingerly in her head, Jenna knew what she would do next. It was a sunny, Sunday morning and Jenna snuck out of the bed she shared with Nathaniel. Quietly, she tip-toed out of the bedroom. It wasn't often the two of them had the entire day off together. They were both seniors at Marlboro college and were interning at Brattleboro Memorial Hospital. With college and work there were few hours left to truly enjoy themselves. This morning, Jenna wanted to surprise Nathan by making him breakfast in bed. She had just put on the water to make a pot of coffee when she heard the lock of the front door start to turn. With a ceramic coffee mug in hand she turned to face the door.

30

Hector stopped in town and picked up a half a dozen bagels along with a small tub of cream cheese. People who were in line, stepped out to let him to the front. The sooner he got what he needed the less they would have to look at him. Hector was used to this treatment by now and quickly placed his order while trying to ignore the looks of the horrified workers behind the counter. As fast as possible they got his bagels together along with the cream cheese, took his cash, and sent him on his way. Hector made the short drive back and pulled into the driveway of his son's cabin. This cabin was in much better shape than the one he owned when he purchased the land. Having had it built from scratch and with all new furnishings, it was only the best for his boy. Hector, exited the Wrangler, made his way to the front porch, bent down and took the key that Nathaniel had always left under the rear leg of the rocking chair. He put the key in the lock and turned it. He walked into the living room and as he made his way toward the kitchen, he was greeted by the loudest scream he had ever heard.

31

Jenna's first instinct had her jump back in which she slammed her lower back into the sink, causing her to drop the mug, shattering it into small ceramic pieces. The next normal reaction to what she was seeing was to scream like she had never screamed before, "HELP! Nathan, HELP ME!" Jenna scrambled with her hands behind her back in search of the butcher block of knives. Having finally brushed up against it, and in her desperate struggle to remain calm, she took hold of the largest knife and pointed it out in front of her continually yelling, "Don't come....any ......closer you....YOU monster! I swear before God I'll stab you to death! Stay back you beast!"

Hector was in complete shock as to what was happening

right before his eyes. This young girl dressed in only a short nightgown was totally going berserk. He was speechless. He dared not take another step closer and only hoped her screaming out to his son would put this all in prospective.

Nathaniel was in a deep slumber when he was startled awake by his girlfriend's life piercing blood curdling scream. He sprung up so fast and jumped out of bed in only his boxers and bee lined it straight down the hall and into the kitchen. He stopped dead in his tracks. Jenna was visibly shaking by the intruder who stood only inches away from the front door. The man stared over in the direction of his son with pleading eyes, waiting for an introduction to break this whole ordeal form continuing. Nathaniel first glanced at Jenna, who appeared to now be in shock as well, and then over to the man Nathaniel knew as his dad. Confused by what he was witnessing, and knowing what he was about to do would change his life forever, Nathaniel braced himself for the hardest lie ever. Jenna would never be able to look his father in the eyes like most others and it was too late to try and change the outcome. So, with only a moment to spare, Nathaniel turned and faced his father, "I'm only going to say this once. Turn around and leave now, and I won't call the police. You HEAR me? Get off these premises right now and I'll let you leave in peace. And if you ever step foot near my property again, I'll have you locked up for good." He then went over to Jenna and wrapped her up in his arms while she buried her face into his shoulders, weeping uncontrollably. Nathaniel held her tightly as he watched his father, the man who would give up his last breath of air for him, slowly leave the cabin. It wasn't until the front door closed that Nathaniel shed a tear for the man he would always love.

Hector heard what his son was saying and thought he

was having an out of body experience. Could this really be happening to him? Had his son really chosen to pretend he was a stranger or no less an intruder into the cabin he had built for him. Slowly with tears forming in his eyes, Hector backed up to the front door, never taking his eyes off his son. The son he worshipped more than life itself. The son who chose a girl over his own flesh and blood. Even if he tried to speak, Hector couldn't. He felt his vocal cords were paralyzed and was left speechless. All he could think to do was back out of the cabin and hope that his son would come to his senses and wrong this mess that had taken place. Hector left the cabin with the bag of bagels in tow and somehow managed to drive the mile back to his own cabin without remembering how he did.

32

"I'm so sorry Nathan, I just can't stay here. What if one day while you're at school or even at the hospital he comes back. I would die if I saw that face again. Bad as it is, I'll probably have nightmares for weeks to come."

Nathaniel had finally calmed her down but still didn't have the courage to tell her the truth as to who that disfigured man was. He sensed she was still in a mild state of panic and as he sat on the couch next to her said, "So, what do you suggest we do? Just pack up and leave this very day. And go where?"

With a look of determination in her eyes, she answered, "One of my colleagues told me there is a studio half way between Marlboro college and Brattleboro Memorial. We don't need all this space anyhow. Together we can manage the rent and it would be a whole new experience for us. Please, Nathan if you really really love me, take me away from here. Just the thought of that creature lurking out there somewhere terrifies me."

Nathaniel did love Jenna with all his heart and knew he would do anything for this girl who would one day be his wife. Besides, it was too late to undo the damage to a relationship that would never be the same. Nathaniel betrayed his father and for that the guilt would always be with him. A guilt that would last all of his life. Nathaniel made a promise to himself at that moment. He promised to make up for his betrayal of his father. He would become the best doctor he could and help bring new life into this world whenever he could, even though he might be a failure in his father's eyes. As he looked directly into Jenna eyes, he answered with the utmost passion he could, "I say we get to packing up what we really need and getting out of this place once and for all."

33

Hector sat for what felt like years each day in his recliner replaying over and over the thought that if he did things differently, his son would still be calling him to check in. Why he didn't stop the young girl from screaming by saying who he really was, still puzzled him. Hector guessed the fact that he didn't know Nathaniel had a girlfriend, evidently living with him, took him by surprise. He kept reliving the scene and each time the results were the same. The young girl freaked out by his appearance, he couldn't utter a sound, and his son denounced him. It had now been three weeks and Hector had never gone this long without a call from Nathaniel. After the second week, Hector tried twice to call him in hopes he would pick up but he never did. Even after all Nathaniel did that Sunday morning, Hector forgave him. He needed his son in his life. He gave a lot of thought to what he was about to do and he hoped the outcome would resolve the tension Nathaniel and the young girl may have had since that terrible experience. Hector went into the spare bedroom that had been Nathaniel's and went into his closet. Hidden in the back was the large duffle bag of the settlement money he once received. Hector no longer cared about this money. He wanted to give it all to his son in hopes his son would come back into his life. Throughout the years, Hector was careful and sometimes downright frugal when it came to spending the $2.1 million he received. The interest alone from the few years at the bank brought in enough to cover the cars, the cabin and property, the newly built cabin and even his son's college education. He barely put a dent in the original payout from the oil company. He estimated by keeping a log that there was still close to the $2 million still intact. Hector rummaged through the bag taking out a few stacks of hundreds for himself just to barely get by in case he lived into his golden years. The rest he would give his son. An amount that still totaled close to 1.7 million. From most of the shows on television it appeared that greed was the way the world operated. He would buy back his son even if it cost him his fortune. So with the remaining fortune he had left, he got into his jeep once again and set off to make things right.

34

As soon as Hector pulled up in front of the log cabin, he felt something wasn't right. A deep knot twisted in his stomach.

Something was amiss. Slowly he opened the driver's door and stepped down on the running board and out of the jeep. He made his way briskly to where he knew Nathaniel kept the spare key. As luck would have it the key was there. This time to play it very safe he knocked repeatedly. Softer at first and then even harder. He was prepared to offer his son all the money Nathaniel could ever dream of spending in his lifetime. All Hector wanted was to have the loving relationship they had back. Hector unlocked the door, with the duffle bag in hand, and after no one answered his constant banging prepared to enter. As soon as he stepped in, the knot he had first experienced tightened even more. Hector looked around. The place was deserted and it looked as if the occupants left in a hurry. Scattered about were open kitchen drawers and cabinets and after surveying the other rooms, his suspicions were confirmed. His son left in a heartbeat. Packed up what he could and just left. That was why there were no phone calls inbound or outbound. Nathaniel had deserted him once and for all. Hector was heartbroken. He stood there in the living room when suddenly he noticed an envelope left on one of the end tables. He quickly rushed over and picked it up tearing the back flap open. He recognized the handwriting right away. It was a letter from Nathaniel to him. Hector sat himself down on the couch and started to read it:

> *Dearest Dad,*
>
> *I hope that you have found this letter as it was the most difficult thing for me to ever write. There is no explaining why I did what I did. I will have to live with that decision forever. I love Jenna and meant to introduce you, but I always was fearful of the outcome. This was not the outcome*

I had hoped for but it is the one I chose to live with. There will never be a day in my life that I won't feel my betrayal of you. I'll have to learn to live with that too. I never looked at you like most people do. You were just my dad. The father who raised me and loved me. The man I didn't have the courage to introduce to my future wife. Even now as I sneak to write this, Jenna is packing up our belongings. I am leaving this cabin and everything else behind. That includes you as well. Forgive me father for I know I have sinned. I will love you until the day I die. Please don't try to find me as I will not come back for you. As much as it breaks my heart, I will have to live with it broken forever.

Your loving but despicable son,
Nathaniel

Hector sat there for the remainder of the day and into the night. When he was finally able to compose himself, he stood up and put the letter now folded in half into his coat pocket. Nathaniel, his loving son, had disowned him. He didn't ever want to see him again. What had just moments ago been self-pity had suddenly turned to a rage Hector hadn't experienced since the loss of Millie. First the loss of his wife and now his son. One by death and the other by choice. Hector started to pace around the room with his fists clenched. He wanted to punch a wall. As he started to head over to one, he nearly tripped over the duffle bag. The duffle bag of money. Money that would never bring back Millie and now his son. His blood was boiling over. He needed to take a deep breath. It was in that instant when he closed his eyes, he had a flashback of that woman.

Ed's momma, whose name from so many years prior, had since slipped his memory. By the grace of God, whom he no longer believed in, Hector should have handed the entire settlement to her. After all, he was the cause of the accident and never admitted to it. The money was indeed hers and it was as if she knew deep down, that was the case and why she showed up at his doorstep. Hector refused to even give her one cent of it and remembered hearing her whimpering some sort of spell or curse upon him. Then like a ton of bricks just hit him, he snapped out of the memory. The woman cursed him or at least put some sort of curse on this money. He remembered her saying nothing good would ever follow him. Since then nothing good had come his way. He lost his beloved Millie at childbirth and now his son deserted him for good. Although Hector had planned to leave most of his money to his son, he no longer wanted it himself. His life had been cursed by it and every day just looking in the mirror proved it. Perhaps if he did give the woman money back then, Millie may have still been alive. Hector was no longer angry. In place of the rage moments before, now tears were streaming down his cheeks. He took the sleeve of his coat to wipe them away but they wouldn't stop. He reached down and took the handle of the duffle bag and headed to the small pantry off the kitchen. He shoved the duffle bag toward the back corner and closed the door. He never wanted to use that money again. He would only use what he took before to help him live out his existence. Hector then headed out the front door of the cabin realizing that this door could remain closed forever as well. He stepped out onto the porch and looked up to the heavens. A heaven he was still uncertain really existed and if it did, Millie was surly there. While the tears still streamed down his face, he mouthed the only word he could possibly think of, "WHY?"

35

As Hector laid there now fully awake, he pondered just why after all these years did he think back to all those painful memories. He assumed it must be tied to the fact that his gut instinct told him the duffle bag had been found. Let that motley crew deal with the cursed money. He didn't care to ever use it again. He thought it odd he had been renting out Nathaniel's cabin these last seven seasons, that no one else had stumbled upon the money. Then again, he never ventured out to meet the renters as he had this time. He deserved the treatment he received. He hadn't touched the inside of the cabin in over thirty years and left it exactly as it was from years past, when Nathaniel left and never looked back. Hector had never expected to live as long as he did and his income from the money he did keep had dwindled down to nothing. Hector had since learned how to google his way around the internet and soon learned that through Craig's list he could rent it out and never have to meet the people to do so. They would send him a check and he would leave them the key in the same spot Nathaniel had in the past. A few of the renters politely asked for some of their money back claiming they didn't realize the cabin had never been updated, but Hector said he was too old to make renovations. Apparently, the people accepted that but in return never rented the cabin from him again. Each season was a different group of people. This was the first group he had ever met and the outcome was exactly as it always was. People stared at him like he wasn't human. Just once Hector, even as an old man now, wished people could accept him for who he was and not what he looked like.

Hector decided he needed to use the bathroom. He slowly lifted his legs off the side of the bed, stood, and walked the distance. He switched on the bathroom light and looked in the mirror. Hector smiled. He smiled for the first time in many years. Even as grotesque as the image that stared back, he continued to smile. Hector knew as he knew that he breathed in fresh air that the cursed money had indeed been found. Let them take it off his hands once and for all, and let them too, suffer the fate that he once endured.

Part II

THE AGREEMENT

36

Meghan had sipped the last of her champagne while the three guys had already guzzled theirs down and already cracked open some beers. "Is it me or has Danielle been gone forever?," she said to no one in particular.

"I was just thinking the same thing," Kimberly chimed in. "How long does it take to find a broom or dust pan?"

Rather than call out Danielle's name, Meghan decided to just take a quick peek in the pantry. If Freddie wasn't drinking a beer a few feet away, Meghan would have bet they were in the room fucking. They were the horniest couple she knew. They practically fucked anywhere they could. Once Danielle confided in Meghan that they did it between book rows in a public library. Patrons were sitting just feet away in chairs reading while Freddie leaned her up against the bookcase and entered her from behind. They were insatiable when it came to sex. She had wished she were more like Danielle in that sense. Her and Cole had been trying to have a baby the last few years and it was causing stress on both of them. Sex was no longer pleasurable for them as it had become more of a chore than a desirable act. Each month while she was ovulating, she would stop Cole from whatever he was doing and insist right then and there that he perform on cue. The actual art of lovemaking was now a sort of ritual for impregnating his wife. Maybe this weekend would be the one since she knew her eggs were fertile. Meghan had reached the small door and opened it a bit suddenly. She didn't realize she was so quiet until she opened the pantry door and startled Danielle. Danielle was hunched over what appeared to look like wads of money. As soon as Danielle saw Meghan, she quickly leaned over the bag, covering what Meghan now knew was money. And from the fast glance that Meghan did see, it looked as if there was more money than her eyes could take in.

"Is that what I think it is?," Meghan asked of her best friend. "My God. Is that wads of money you were just holding."

"Don't be silly. What money?," Danielle replied nervously. "I was just closing up this bag and coming out to tell you all that I couldn't find anything to sweep up that glass. Don't you think if there was money I would have called for someone to get in here."

"I don't know Danielle, would you? From the looks of it, you were contemplating something since you were in here so long. Whether or not that included the rest of us, I'm not so certain. Open the bag and let me see."

Danielle hesitated but finally started to unzip the duffle bag again. As soon as she did, Meghan gasped when it was fully opened. "Holy, mother of GOD! Is that stuffed full with bills? How? Where?," Meghan kept repeating over and over in disbelief.

"Yes, okay. It is money and its mine!," Danielle answered with a snippy tone.

"Are you for real? Yours? And why is that?"

"Well first off, I was the one to come in here and find it. It was buried in the back corner," she pointed to the spot where she pulled it out from. "No one else would have come in here if I didn't drop the glass. So technically it is mine," Danielle now spoke more confidently.

"Really. I can't believe you. We'll just have to see about that!," Meghan's voice started to rise as she took hold of one handle of the duffle bag and started to pull it from the pantry.

"Hey, cut the shit Meg! It's mine!!," as she grabbed hold of the other handle being dragged along.

Meghan opened the door but was barely able to pull the bag because of its weight. Danielle at this point had given up and wanted to be out of this confined pantry and pulled the other handle with Meghan. Slowly they emerged from the room and into the kitchen as Kimberly and the guys all stared over at them.

Kimberly spoke first, "What in the name of mercy have you two girls got in there?"

"Looks like they are carrying a body," Matt chimed in.

"Hopefully the body of that old geezer, what's his name again Stevie Skeevie?" laughed Freddie.

"Stop it Freddie. His name is Hector Skeeve. And for God's sake, have some sympathy for the old man," With the bag in tow, Meghan started to perspire from the effort made in lugging the heavy bag.

As soon as the girls dropped the bag, Freddie sprinted over and unzipped it not a moment too soon. He reached in and pulled out a few stacks of bills. "Whoa ho ho! What the FUCK is this? Did you find this Danny baby?" This was a term Freddie used whenever he was trying to butter up his new bride.

"As a matter of fact I did? And Meghan said it's not mine."

"And who the fuck made her commander in chief? If you found it, it sure as shit is OURS!," Freddie said in his overly accented Spanish. "This bag of mother fucking money is ours and we are RICH. Fucking, filthy RICH!"

Cole had heard enough from Freddie, "Easy there Freddie. Who said the money is yours or anyone else's for that matter? It belongs to the owner of this cabin. Don't you think he'll see its missing and know we took it?"

Danielle interjected, "The duffle bag was hidden in a corner and covered in dust. I don't think it's been looked at in years."

Freddie was getting agitated, "And there you go with the 'we took it'. Who the fuck said its yours? And as far as that old man goes, I bet he doesn't even know it exists from what my Danny baby is saying. So yes technically we found it so it's his loss."

Matt decided to jump in, "Dude, are you fucking crazy? That's stealing man. We could get locked up for that. Besides, who knows where it came from. Maybe the old dude robbed some banks back in his day."

"And he wouldn't have needed a mask that's for sure. Danielle and I are keeping it and to hell with the rest of you. In other words, fuck off!"

"Ease up there Mister big shot talker. Watch your language in front of the ladies. There are also many legalities to consider as well. We don't need to wind up in jail," Cole said.

Kimberly was astonished by how this was all unfolding in front of her eyes. It was just minutes ago she and the girls were hopping around like silly bunnies to the guys roaring laughter and now Freddie was acting like a madman over a sack full of money that wasn't his. "Cole's right. Let's all sit down and talk about this."

"Fuck talking, this shit is mine. Like it or not bitch, I'm keeping it," Freddie glared over at Kimberly as he finished.

Matt couldn't believe Freddie called his wife a bitch and started to approach Freddie. He pushed him in the chest. "And who the fuck do YOU thinking you're calling a bitch? Dude, all kidding aside, I'll knock the shit out of you if you ever call my wife a bitch, joking or not." He pushed Freddie against the wall. Freddie lunged at Matt. Although Matt was much taller than Freddie, the blow caught him in the stomach briefly knocking the wind out of Matt. Matt stumbled back, caught his breath again and went at Freddie full force. The two of them were hurling punches mid-air and missing each other completely. Before Cole interceded, Freddie took one last swing and caught Matt on his lower lip, cutting the lip open. Blood started to ooze out. Matt pulled back his arm and let a punch go directly to his face, hitting Freddie square in the nose and instantly his nose started to bleed. Cole forced his way in between them and with both his arms outstretched, kept them apart.

"Knock it off you two! You're being a complete asshole Freddie. You hear me Freddie, A COMPLETE ASSHOLE!!," Cole shouted while still holding them at an arm's length.

Danielle, who now wished she hadn't come across the bag, was watching this mayhem before her, started crying, "Stop it! Please stop it." She sunk down on her knees and crawled over to Freddie. "Are you okay?" She took the sleeve of her pajamas and dabbed at his bleeding nose. The blood was dripping down his chin and onto the front of his shirt. Kimberly ran over to the sink and grabbed some paper towels. She turned on the faucet and wet the towels. She walked over to Danielle and gave her a few pieces and with the remaining, she stood next to Matt and put some pressure on his lip. She held her fingers on the towel for a minute or so and when she looked at the cut she said, "Well, at least it isn't a deep cut or we all may have had to head over to the nearest hospital for stitches. Your bottom teeth just nicked the top of your lip. It could have been a lot worse. Really, everyone. Was that necessary? I know you were defending my honor Matt and I appreciate it, but we're all FRIENDS. Long-time friends. Not complete strangers."

Meghan had been holding her tongue the whole time and now felt the time was right, "We ALL need to calm ourselves the fuck and excuse my language DOWN! What the hell just happened? Like we all saw this money and it turned us into lunatics. Listen, Danielle, your right. You did find it but in all actuality it isn't yours or anyone else's for that matter. We only rented this cabin for three nights. And from the looks of that bag this money has been here for quite some time. We should just tell Mr. Skeeve and let him decide......"

Danielle, who had since soothed Freddie down a bit, interrupted Meghan, "And what? Hand over a bag of money and say, 'Oh by the way we found this bag buried in your pantry.' Seriously, Meghan, let's just keep it. Yes, Freddie, Danny baby wants us ALL to keep it. My God, what WAS I thinking. I was so numb when I first saw all that cash and all these thoughts were running through my head. You and Kimberly ARE my two closest friends for life and that is what is important. Besides we don't even know how much cash is in this bag."

Freddie moved Danielle's hand off his nose and still seething from the confrontation with Matt said, "But Danny baby, after all you were the one who found it. I say you give this some serious thought before you....."

Now Danielle interjected, "I made up my mind and that is final. These are my girls. My girls Freddie. Gosh, do you even fucking realize what we three have been through since we met. School girl crushes, our first periods, breaking curfews, losing our grandparents. And we were ALWAYS there for one another. Remember girls when we were in fourth grade and we camped out in your backyard in that tent that smelled like mildew from being in your damp unfinished basement Meghan?"

Meghan started to laugh, "Yes, my mom used to yell at my father for keeping it down there. Oh, and remember we got so scared when we heard a racoon, and it came right up to the zipper on the outside of the tent, that we all started to scream."

"Yeah, like we were being killed and your dad thought we were being attacked by a rapist or something and ran out in his boxers," Kimberly said as all three started to laugh even harder.

"Oh, my God, I forgot about that," Meghan said after catching her breath from laughing so hard. "After my father saw the racoon running away and that we were fine, he tried to cover himself up and we starting laughing. He was wearing some super hero boxers. My mom brought them as a gag gift for his birthday but he loved them."

"Yes, yes, they were um, um the Incredible Hulk green ones!," Kimberly said as she snorted.

"That's right!," Meghan agreed. "Wow, what a great memory."

"See, this is what I mean," Danielle continued. "That same night we all said what we would do if we ever became rich and famous and do you remember what each one of us said?"

Both Meghan and Kimberly shook their heads in agreement.

"That if one of us became rich, we would take care of the other two and vice versa."

Now Freddie started laughing in a pissed off way and no longer referring to her as Danny baby, "Really, Danielle? You want to keep a pact you all made when you were like......like," he became embarrassed that all eyes were now on him and said, "what? fucking nine-year old virgins."

Ignoring her husband's last stupid comment, Danielle decided to approach the money from a different angle, "I say we at least count it and see just how much there is. Maybe we can take just some. What do ya say? It'll be fun."

Freddie instantly agreed with his wife.

"I guess it wouldn't hurt just to see how much we are talking about," chimed in Kimberly.

"I'll go for that. What's the harm?," Matt said next.

"Then I'll second that too," Cole said as he stood over by Meghan.

Meghan, still looking uncomfortable, tried to once again reason with them, "But it isn't ours. What's the use of counting it if we don't have any intention of keeping it. Seems like just a waste of time. Besides, I thought you guys were STARVING."

"Dinner isn't going anywhere honey. Might be fun just to see just how much there is crammed into this bag. All those in favor of waiting to eat and counting some cash raise your hands," Cole asked as his hand was the first up in the air.

Immediately, Freddie put his hand up, followed by Kimberly and Danielle a second thereafter. Matt was next. Meghan looked over as all five had their hands raised and slowly and with a tad of guilt raised hers last smiling as she said, "Excuse me again, but why the fuck not."

All six of them started laughing and Matt walked over to the bag at the same time as Freddie, and together they lifted the bag with ease to place it on the kitchen table, to start counting.

Feeling like a complete jerk and knowing he did indeed need to apologize to them all, Freddie spoke in language they were used to and said, "Sorry for being such an ASSHOLE about this whole thing. I guess I am a big DICK at times too. Didn't mean to bust your lip Matt. I hope we can leave this behind us."

"Apology accepted. And yes, you were a BIG DICK, but I was a dick as well. Sorry about your nose. I'm glad it's not broken. Caught you more on the cheek. Consider this whole thing forgotten. Now let's get our fingers working as we sort out all this money."

All six of them shook their heads in agreement and the

ordeal was now behind them as they each took a seat at the table to start counting. Freddie reached into the duffle bag and distributed a few stacks to each and the process had begun. Before taking her own seat, Kimberly grabbed a pen and pad from a kitchen drawer to write down the figures from each bundle. Together, all six sat silently each opening a strap and counting their bills. Each one of them pondering to themselves, just how good their lives would be if they did decided to keep the money. But in keeping the money, the price they might have to pay would be costly.

37

"Wait, let me just add these last three totals together," Kimberly said as she punched in numbers on the calculator of her phone. "Are you all ready for this? A whopping grand total of $1.566 million….. 1.566 million dollars."

"No fucking way! Really?," Matt asked again.

"Yes, really. I triple checked it. I added all our figures each separately and then as one complete column. I do know how to add up numbers."

"That is a shit load of moolah. We're filthy rich!" Freddie added.

"Whoa, I thought we were just counting the money. No one said anything about keeping it. Besides, it took us close to two hours and now all that food we were starving for is cold. Truth be told, I even lost my appetite." Meghan stated.

"Makes two of us," Danielle admitted as well. "We really need to consider the options here. If we were to split it three ways, how much are we looking at?"

"A little over a half million each. It works out to be $522,000 for each couple to be precise," Cole confirmed as he held up his phone showing the total.

"And that ain't chump change if you ask me. I say we take our chances. Fuck the old man. Probably doesn't even remember he had it. Let's divvy it up and get the hell out of here," insisted Freddie.

Cole, being the most practical of the group made a very strong point, "Listen. We came up here to ski and have some much needed fun in our stress filled lives. For now, let's not make rash decisions. Let's heat up the food, drink some beers, and sleep on it. We can take a vote in the morning to determine what we decide to do. Freddie has a valid point. The old man may just have forgotten about the money. Even if he does realize, who's to say when he will. He may never. He could even die and then what? Someone else may come into the cabin to clear out his things and stumble across it. And then they keep it. Again, I say we just seriously all talk about it after a good night's rest. What do ya say?"

Matt didn't let a second pass before he added, "You can tell who the lawyer is. He has me convinced already." The others all burst out laughing as they, too, agreed that Cole, the lawyer, may very well have just convinced them all of the most obvious choice, and won this case hands down.

38

Each of them sat around the table picking at their food. Just hours prior, Cole, Matt and Freddie were starving savages ready to tear into the London broil. Now even the guys barely touched the meat. Their thoughts were consumed by the duffle bag stuffed with over one point five million plus dollars. A half million for each couple. Money that could and would change each of their lives drastically. Cole was deep in thought. He and Meghan had purchased a home and were trying to start a family. Cole had hoped to one day start his own law firm. This money could help him pay off his loans, put some money in their savings account and open his own practice. Kimberly picked at her plate. She used her fork to move around her food to make it look like she was eating, as she too, had no real appetite. She kept thinking of that bag full of cash. Even though Kimberly loved Matt's Aunt Mary, her one desire was always having dreamt of owning their own home. Being a paralegal paid well but she, too, wanted to have kids of her own. Matt, the avid surfer, worked as a bartender during the winter months. The tips were good and he was very well liked by his customers but all in all people didn't drink like they used to. Law enforcement officers were cracking down on drunk drivers and people were afraid to drink and drive. Kimberly knew that splitting the money would enable them to buy their own home and get them on their feet. Meanwhile, Danielle sat there staring over at her two best friends. Deep down she knew that she and Kimberly would opt for the money. Meghan, on the other hand, might hold out. She was always the miss goody two shoes. Always doing the right thing for the right cause. Now, she was hoping that Cole would be able to persuade her to join the group and decide to keep the money. Although she enjoyed her job as a beautician, she was getting tired of listening to all her women customers from the south of Merrick road in Merrick brag about this purchase or just how much this item cost. With a half million dollars of their own, perhaps she could open her own salon and have Freddie start his own repair shop. Freddie could be the boss and hire his own mechanics to perform the work. Danielle secretly played Lotto and Mega Millions each week. She only played the minimum amount for each. She knew if she told Freddie, he would just laugh at her and tell her she was wasting her money. But deep down Danielle always believed that all it took was a dollar and a dream. And right now, she wasn't dreaming that a half million dollars could be hers. All they all had to do was agree on keeping the cash. Make a pact on the agreement. As simple as that. What she didn't realize was that some dreams can become nightmares.

39

It was close to midnight and the conversations around the table were far and few between. What was always a flowing stream of many topics going on at once, was now barely a single sentence that any of them responded to. Cole pushed back his chair and stood up, "Well, I guess I'll call it a night. I want to be up by six thirty to be on the lift line and ready to go when they open. And, some of you need to rent skis and that may take some time."

No one said anything in return. They each got up from their seat and said their goodnights before heading into their separate bedrooms. The money was heavily weighing on their minds and clouded any reasonable sense of thoughts at the moment.

"I'll knock on your doors bright and early so no one

oversleeps," Cole reassured them all as he walked into the master bedroom, closing the door behind him.

Since Meghan was already in her bunny pajama's, she was innocently snooping through the nightstand drawers. She pulled out a card with a heart on it.

"Are you looking for some more cash in there?," Cole inquired with a sly grin. He had since stripped down to his boxers and was getting into the bed next to Meghan.

"Ha, ha very funny. I really don't know why I went through these drawers. Curiosity I guess. You just never know. And if I know Kimberly and especially Danielle, they are doing exactly the same thing." Meghan opened the card and read it. "Why would someone leave a card that is filled with such admiration and love for someone behind?" She started to read a bit of it,

'Dear Nathan,

I know you love the name Nathaniel and almost everyone we know calls you that, but I want to be different. As you told me time and time again, your name means Gift of God. Well YOU are a gift. My gift. And as I like to call you Nathan to be different, is just like how our love is different than most. From the moment I saw you in that off the beaten path little cafeteria in college, I knew you were special. And now look, just a few weeks later and we are living together and life is the best. I mean the total BEST! Not only do I love you with all my heart but I admire your stamina in the hospital as well as in the sheets. Wink, wink………'

"Nice, and speaking of stamina, how 'bout I show you mine," Cole said patting the mattress with his hand.

Meghan turned her body in his direction and pressed her body up against his. Cole leaned over and kissed her first gently on the lips. Meghan opened her mouth and once their tongues met, he passionately kissed her again. He rolled on top of her and she slid her hands into his boxers and squeezed his ass before helping him ease them off. Cole was hungry for her. He unzipped her pajamas and took them off her shoulders, sucking and licking each nipple as he did. She helped him slide them off and pushed them to the floor with her feet. He continued lapping at her breasts. In a moment of pure ecstasy, Meghan moaned out loud not caring that her two girlfriends and their husbands were within hearing distance. For once, she didn't care if she got pregnant. She, too, had this wild animal extinct taking over her body. She reached down and took hold of Cole's fairly larger than average penis and guided it into her moist vagina. Within seconds Cole was pumping harder than he had in their last few love makings. Meghan didn't know if the money sparked some sort of fire within them. She couldn't get enough of Cole inside her and with his every thrust, she matched him stroke for stroke. Each time he pushed deeper inside her, she arched her back to meet his push. She was screaming out now in pleasure. What felt like they were screwing for a while, lasted only five minutes. Cole was sweating and it was dripping off his forehead. Meghan felt his back and that, too, was dripping with perspiration. Cole was getting close to releasing his manhood deep within her and Meghan was very close to orgasm as well. Together they climaxed like they hadn't in months. Totally drained and relaxed, they both were asleep in minutes.

"Looks like someone got satiated," laughed Kimberly. "I didn't think Meghan could be so vocal. She used to tell Danielle and I that whenever she fucked, she was as quiet as a mouse."

"From the sounds of her squealing, I'd say more like Minnie Mouse." Matt, who at 6' was only a few inches taller than his wife. He had since stripped down to his boxer briefs. With his blonde hair and blue eyes he was every bit the envy of most other men. Kimberly often noticed how other women would turn their heads and stare him up and down, wishing he were theirs instead of hers. Kimberly all of a sudden felt a wetness between her legs. It had been a while since Matt and she really got it on. It wasn't that Matt didn't turn her on, his body was a sculptured masterpiece along with his enormous tool of a dick. Kimberly wanted him and she wanted him badly. She walked over to him and pushed him onto the bed. Before he knew what was going on, she knelt before him, quickly took his boxer briefs down and off his ankles, and took his cock in her mouth. Within seconds he was instantly hard. Harder than he had been in quite some time. He felt his penis throb with every sucking motion Kimberly entertained. Matt leaned his elbows onto the bed and watched his wife work his organ. He couldn't remember the last time that his wife performed fellatio on him, nor would he question why out of the blue now. He did know that he was getting close to releasing his load. He, too, had now wanted her so badly. Pushing off his elbows, he took hold of her head enough so that he was able to release his cock out of her mouth. With his penis as erect as it was he pulled her up with both hands and spun her around. Kimberly unzipped her pajamas as Matt practically ripped them off of her. He then pushed her onto the bed, as he took hold of her buttocks and pulled her to the edge with her ass a bit off the mattress. Quickly, he inserted his cock deep within her and started pumping with a ferocity that he hadn't felt in a while. As he pumped faster and deeper within her, he leaned his chest onto her back and cupped her breasts at the same time. Kimberly brushed back her short black hair that kept falling in front of her eyes. Dripping with sweat, it was now matted and no longer would move. They were like two wild animals in heat. It was only moments before she was telling Matt just how loud Meghan was. And now together as one, they both had their own intense orgasm, as Matt howled out loud like a coyote.

"Jesus, are we the only two that haven't fucked yet?," Danielle said to Freddie who was standing in front of her buck naked. Freddie had enjoyed sleeping in the buff. "Aren't we supposed to be the lovebirds? First Meghan calling out and now Matt howling. What is wrong with this picture?"

"Well, I'm sure the fuck positive I can change all that," Freddie answered as his cock started to become erect. For such a short man at only 5'2", his dick was nicely proportioned. Freddie was her hair bear. Dark hair covered his chest and stomach. His ass was also covered in black hair and a bit more hairy than she liked. Over the summers, whenever the six of them would head to Robert Moses beach for the day, she noticed just how hairless Matt and Cole were compared to her husband. Matt was so totally hairless, that she swore Kimberly had a hairier body than his with her dark hair and all. Cole had a light brown peach fuzz on his chest and legs and on occasion had sometimes had Danielle wishing that Freddie looked like that. Freddie, she noticed, didn't care one way or the other how hairy he was. And if he was comfortable with his body that was really all that mattered. Freddie slowly climbed the ladder of the bunks beds. Once he was situated up top, he called down for Danielle to join him. As Danielle watched him make his way up the wood rungs of the ladder, she started to slowly get turned on. Seeing his hairy ass make its way up, instantly sent a shiver down her body. Danielle reached her hand into the zipper of her pajama and cupped her own breast. With her other hand, she undid the whole zipper and stepped out of the footsies. With just a light pink thong on, she slowly let her hand slide off her breasts and onto the trimmed hair of her vagina. Danielle didn't know what had come over her. She inserted her index finger inside of her and moaned slightly. Freddie, lying flat on his back, now leaned his head over the side and watched as she moved her body to the rhythm of her hand. He took hold of his own cock and started to stroke it up and down. Danielle was far enough back to see what he was doing and it turned her on even more. She took her two fingers that she had since placed inside her out and walked over to the ladder. She was up and on top of Freddie's cock in no time flat. She placed her hands up on the ceiling, now moaning just as loud as the others, and with her head thrown back, rode him like there was no tomorrow.

40

One by one, they each entered the kitchen groggy eyed and bushy tailed. Meghan had put on a fresh pot of coffee and was sitting at the table looking at her Facebook page. Cole had scrambled a dozen eggs and sizzled a whole pound of bacon. He was mixing in shredded cheese to the eggs and was getting ready to take the hash browns off the stove. With a hearty breakfast in them, they would be good to go until the afternoon, when they would stop for lunch at the lodge. Kimberly along with Matt joined them next. Danielle entered the kitchen and Freddie followed stretching his arms up in the air as he did, "I don't know about the rest of you, but last night was some trip."

Matt agreed and said, "You can say that again. Wasn't there some song in the seventies that went like….." And in his Californian accent sang, "Oh what a night. Late December back in '63 What a very special time for me, as I remember what a night……."

Danielle, the most outspoken with regard to her sexuality of the three girls, was about to catch them all off guard by saying, "Yeah, girls. It was like I was some sort of sex vixen. I couldn't get enough of it. I think we fucked for at least an hour and a half straight. My back is killing me from riding Freddie. It's as stiff as his……."

"TMI…….please way too much information," Kimberly stopped her from going into any more details than necessary. "I felt like I was sexually possessed too but I'm not sharing any details."

Freddie laughed and said, "Yeah someone was howling

at the moon from your room Kimberly. And a lot of moaning and groaning coming from the other one."

Meghan who normally would never participate in such a conversation decided to join in this time by adding, "Never mind what we heard or didn't hear. The point is, it was as if the money had us all kinked out. Like it made us all sexually crazy. Perhaps just another reason we shouldn't keep it."

"And why the hell not? If keeping that money makes us all the more happier to fuck, which is what it did to us all by putting us all in a euphoric state. Let's split that money NOW and worry about the consequences later," demanded Freddie.

Cole had made them each a plate for breakfast and placed one in front of them. As they all dug in with insatiable appetites after their night of passion, he decided to broach the subject again, "So let's get right down to it again. Like I explained last night, it is very risky what we might be considering. And if down the line, we should get caught, we take the fall as a group. No one gets singled out for keeping or not wanting to have kept the money." He glanced over at his wife who he knew needed the most coaxing. "We are in it as one for all and all for one! I say yes let's keep the money and take our chances. Mr. Skeeve is old and doesn't even know it was still there."

"I'm in!," Freddie immediately added.

"You can count us in too," Kimberly answered for both her and Matt. "We discussed it before we came out and figured when are we ever going to come across money like this. We'd be fools not to jump on this opportunity."

The others except Meghan stared over at Danielle who

had just taken a sip of her orange juice, "You bet your sweet asses I'm in. Did you all forget I was the one who found this fortune. Damned if I'm not going to be included."

Both Kimberly and Danielle knew that Meghan was having a difficult time deciding and just let her ponder it in silence for a few minutes. The guys, even Cole, were getting antsy and fidgeting in their seats. Meghan took a bite of her bacon and chewed and chewed until she swallowed finally saying what they all hoped and prayed for, "I'd hate to be the party pooper. Although I'm still not 100% certain this is the right choice, I'd hate to see someone else get their hands on it. So, I'm in!"

The two girls started clapping right away as the guys reached across the table high fiving one another. The atmosphere in the room was giddy from all the laughter that ensued. They had all decided to get an early start on skiing and to divvy up the money later on that evening. Matt and Freddie cleared the table by placing all the dishes in the sink to be washed later. As the three couples all were heading back to their rooms to put on their snow gear for the full day ahead Cole added one last statement as any typical lawyer would by saying, "Since the agreement has been met by all parties involved, I say we now ski the hell out of those mountains."

Part III

THE AFTERMATH

41

"Yo bros, Slow down! You know I ain't that good on these things," begged Freddie as he tried in vain to catch up to Matt and Cole who were skiing circles around him. All, had gone according to Cole's plans. After they finished breakfast, they geared up for a day on the slopes. They piled into the Yukon and were at the base of Mount Snow in less than ten minutes from the cabin. The weather was calling for mild temperatures turning to colder temps by the afternoon. The sky was sunny and bright for most of the morning. The lines for the rentals were as expected since it was a holiday weekend. While the girls and Freddie waited to be fitted for their ski's, Cole and Matt went to purchase the lift tickets. Normally the astronomical price for the lift tickets shocked Cole, but this time he didn't even flinch when he handed over his credit card. Knowing he was getting over a half million dollars by the end of the weekend, made it easier to accept. After getting their skis, boots, poles and helmets, they all met at the first chair lift at the base of the mountain.

The girls were all dressed to the max in their ski outfits decided to ski the easier trails from the top of the mountain. The top of Mount Snow was known as the Summit with an elevation of 3600'. They rode up in the chairlifts with the guys. When they got to the top, the girls skied off to the left to ski down the trails such as Little John and Long John which led into Deer Run. These trails were wide open with room for beginners who may ski out of control, allowing for dangerous collisions to be avoided. The guys chose to start off on intermediate trails like Cascade and Drifter. The lift lines were long and Cole and Matt were a bit pissed that they couldn't get in that many runs in the morning. Before they started their morning, they all agreed to meet at the Summit Lodge on top of the mountain for lunch at 1:30. They chose that time for lunch since most families with small kids stopped earlier, enabling them to get a good hour of less lift lines and consequently more skiing. It was 1:27pm and the girls were already in the lodge having saved a table for them. After the guys took off their skis and placed them together by one of the outdoor posts, they headed inside to find the girls. The girls had already gotten their lunches. It was the usual chicken caesar salad with dressing on the side. They hadn't eaten them yet since they all had promised to wait for one another. Matt and Cole took off their clothes, while Freddie headed straight to the counter to order a burger and fries. Matt and Cole went with the burgers as well as skiing built up an appetite. They also purchased six hot chocolates to warm them up. The temperatures went from a mild 38 degrees down to 26 degrees since they arrived early that morning. Temperatures were expected to go back up later that evening to about 32 degrees with some more snowfall overnight making the conditions great for tomorrow. Cole and Matt made their way back to the table. Once they had all gotten their food and started eating, Danielle who could no longer take it said, "I wish this day was over already. I can't wait to get my hands on all that money."

Meghan immediately replied, "Shush, are you crazy? No talking whatsoever about the money in public and for that matter to anyone else about where we got it. We should all remember to spend it wisely and not go and make any big purchases out of the blue. At least not right away. Now try to contain yourself and let's go and ski some more. The last lift closes at 4 and it is already almost 2:30. I want to get in at least three or four more runs today."

"At the very least three or four. Times a wastin', let's get back on those slopes," Cole commented as he started to get dressed once again.

Again, they rode up together in the chairlifts and followed the same pattern as this morning. The girls went to the left to continue on the green trails for beginners, while the guys hung a right for the more advanced.

"Try to keep up with us Freddie. You said you were an expert when we met you. Seems like we are always hanging back waiting on you," Matt yelled over so both Cole and Freddie could hear.

Cole volunteered which trail they should go down before Matt and Freddie could decide, "Let's do the 'Ledge'. It's been calling out my name all morning."

"Yeah man! Let's do it. We haven't done any black diamonds yet," Matt agreed.

"But black diamonds are for expert skiers. I mean really great expert skiers," Freddie hesitated and started to listen to himself as he sounded quite unconvincing that he was a expert skier. "I mean not that I don't find them challenging and rewarding but we've been skiing all day and our muscles are getting tired."

Matt started to ski toward the 'Ledge' trail with Cole alongside him as he turned back toward Freddie, "Maybe you're tired but I'm just getting started. Cowa bunga dudes, let's tear this baby up!" He then raced off, went over a ridge and was gone in a second.

42

Freddie knew he had bitten off more than he could chew by skiing close enough to the start of 'Ledge'. Now there was no turning back unless he took off his skis to walk back up the mountain to a blue intermediate trail. Black diamonds were way too steep with moguls that had three plus foot drops around each one. It took all of the energy Freddie had left, just to get down half of the mountain. He hadn't seen Matt or Cole for some time now and he was starting to get anxious. He started to snow plow from side to side in areas where he could. His knees were getting shaky and he was losing his confidence. If only he hadn't felt the need to compete with Matt and Cole. They both had been skiing since they were teenagers, while he only started when he met Danielle. He had lied by saying that he took ski lessons and basically had Danielle teach him from scratch. As she was only a beginner herself, it made it much easier for Freddie to take her pointers and accelerate from there. Add in the fact that he was closer to the ground at 5'2", and he perfected his moves rather quickly. In no time flat, he was able to ski intermediate but that was where he felt most comfortable. Take him out of his comfort zone like he was now in, and Freddie would panic. Normally, he could get his techniques in check and his panic would subside, but at this moment in time, he was in full panic alert. Drop after drop and mogul after mogul, he battled the conditions to make it to the bottom. When he was at the last small cliff with smooth sailing from that point on, he spotted Matt and Cole at the base of the trail. They, too, recognized Freddie and waved him on. All he needed to do was clear this ridge and ski straight to the end. There were no more moguls and the trail opened up on each side. In that instant, he felt his panic subside and his confidence creeping back. Deciding he was no longer in any real danger, he gave it all he had, shushing from side to side like an expert skier. Matt and Cole must have been impressed since they both held their poles straight up and looked to be cheering him on. Freddie continued to shush and his speed was increasing, so fast that he didn't have time to avoid the ice patch directly in front of him. Before he knew it, his left ski caught the side of the ice and his right ski went in the opposite direction causing him to split his legs apart. His left ski twisted and so did his legs, causing his right boot to release out of the binding. By then it was too late and Freddie went head over heels tumbling down the mountain until he went over the edge and into a tree, which stopped him abruptly. Matt and Cole couldn't believe what just happened to Freddie. It didn't look good and they both released their boots from the bindings and started running uphill toward him. A group of people were skiing behind Freddie and also witnessed his accident. They were by his side before Matt and Cole had covered much distance. One of their group continued downhill to notify the ski patrol of the accident. Not knowing the severity of his fall, no one touched or tried to move him. They just reassured Freddie that help was on the way. Thankfully, he wore his helmet since he landed inches from the tree. His right leg hit the base of the tree trunk and was twisted at an unusual angle. The people who comforted him could see it was a bad break. Matt and Cole finally made the ascent to the spot where Freddie lay, grimacing in pain. They both knelt down on each side of him and reassured him that he would be fine. They thanked the other skiers who came to his aid and now watched as the Ski Patrol raced up the mountain on two snowmobiles, one of which carried a stretcher. Also, from the top of the mountain came four other ski patrol members who carried knapsacks, certain to contain medicine that would take instant effect. The ski patrols consisted of four young guys and two girls, who told everyone to clear the path and let them do their job. They put a neck brace on him. Then two splints on each leg, twisting his right leg back in place and having Freddie curse using every expletive he knew. By this time, two of the ski patrol guys had placed the stretcher next to him and the other four on the count of three lifted him and placed him securely into it. Matt and Cole watched in horror as their friend, who at times could be a real pain in the ass, was hitched to the back of a snowmobile and whisked away. Matt and Cole told him they would meet at the clinic at the base of Mount Snow. And as they clumsily made their way down the mountain in their boots, they prayed that their friend would be okay.

43

"What do you mean I can't go in the room? That's my fucking husband in there. I want to see him now!," demanded Danielle. Once they got down the mountain, Cole headed directly to the clinic to be with Freddie, while Matt skied over to where he knew the girls would be. In less than five minutes, he spotted all three of them lazily skiing down the mountain. Waving them down, they all skied over to him. Knowing he shouldn't put Danielle in a panic, he said they needed to go to the clinic. Both Meghan and Danielle each pleaded to have Matt tell them which husband was hurt. To put Meghan's mind at ease since she looked terrified it was Cole, he said Freddie took a slight fall. Danielle knew just by the way he said it, that it was more than a minor accident. Again, Matt tried to be evasive about the injury sustained, but before he could finish his next sentence, Danielle skied off in the direction of the clinic. As Matt, Kimberly and Meghan rushed in to the waiting area, there was a scene taking place. Cole was holding onto Danielle as she was screaming she wanted to be with her husband. Both, Meghan and Kimberly took over for Cole, as the nurses tried to explain what was happening. As all five stood outside the surgery room, the head nurse, a robust woman named Tracy, filled them in on exactly what procedures were taking place. The clinic at Mount Snow was better than most other ski resorts. He would be given excellent treatment and since it wasn't a matter of life or death, they would fix his broken leg there. The doctors on staff were highly qualified for any medical emergency. She said that there was no need to get an ambulance to transport Freddie to the nearest hospital. The tibia in his lower leg had broken and needed to be cast. The well-trained doctor on staff was putting the bones back together and a plaster cast would be molded to the leg. Other than that, there were some minor scrapes and bruises. No other broken bones. The nurse said that he should be thankful he was wearing a helmet and that his leg took the brunt of the fall. Once they had casted him, they were going to give him a minor sedative to ease the pain that would follow. Provided they didn't mind waiting a couple of hours for him to wake up, they should be able to take him home later in the evening. He would need to follow up with his primary care physician for a complete physical as a precautionary measure. Danielle had since quieted down as the girls walked her over to the waiting area. Matt and Cole went to return the rental equipment, which of Freddie's, they knew the mountain would be more than happy to refund.

"I can't fucking believe this. I mean, how the hell did he wipe out? I know he insists he is an excellent skier and all, but he CAN hold his own," Danielle said to no one in particular.

"According to the guys, Freddie hit a patch of ice. If you remember the sun was out full force in the morning, melting the snow and then it got real cold and I'm sure froze in some spots. It was an accident. Nothing more and nothing less. Just thank God it was a broken leg and not a head injury. Besides, what did the doctor say, he only has to wear the cast for four to six weeks," Kimberly said reassuring her best friend that all would be fine.

At last the tension broke and Danielle started to giggle, "And do you know what a fucking pain the ass he'll be for the next couple of weeks. I'll need a vacation after that. Bad enough, its Danielle can you get me that or give me this. Imagine with a broken leg. God help me." A God that would do anything but help her in the time to come.

44

It was nearing midnight when the Yukon pulled back in front of the cabin. Both Matt and Cole jumped out and each of them took an arm to help get Freddie down and out of the front passenger seat. They had given him Oxycodone for the pain and Freddie was still a bit drugged. They had to half carry him up the porch steps and into the cabin. They decided to put him in Matt and Kimberly's bed since it would be easier than the bunks. As soon as they laid him down and before Danielle was able to get off his coat and gloves, he had dozed off, presumably from the lingering effects of the drugs. Danielle joined the others in the living room and sat alongside Meghan and Kimberly on the couch.

"I guess we're done with skiing for the weekend," Danielle stated. "I still can't believe this happened. I guess I should be grateful, since it could have been a lot worse."

"That's for sure. It kinda put a damper on the whole weekend if you ask me," Kimberly offered.

Cole looked at all their faces and knew what he must ask next, knowing fully well what their answers would be, "So, what do you all say we try and get a good night's sleep. In the morning, we can make a hearty breakfast. And after that we split up the cash, load it in our bags and head the hell home. I don't feel much like skiing myself as I'm sure we all feel the same."

He watched as one by one they nodded their heads in agreement. All except his wife.

Meghan, once again being the practical one, said, "What about Sunday night? We'll lose our money on this cabin."

Matt, who had been quiet since they got back, answered her the best he knew how, "And with the amount of dough we're talking about, do we really care?"

They all knew what he had just stated was very true and as one, they all burst out laughing.

45

It had been two weeks since their three-day ski weekend fiasco was cut short. As promised all three couples had kept the cash in their homes, as to not raise any flags to how they came across such a large amount of cash. Danielle had been busy all morning tidying up the apartment, since Freddie was anything but a neat freak. After she was finished and it was to her liking, Danielle walked into the living room, where Freddie was sitting on the couch with both his legs up on an ottoman. He had just finished his breakfast that Danielle had prepared and left his plate and coffee cup on the coffee table. He knew she would clean up after him. As she approached him, she was holding two stacks of hundreds. Danielle busily stuffed them in her pocketbook as she mentioned to Freddie, "Don't forget what you promised. You know what today is right?"

Freddie looked from the television show he was just

engrossed in with a puzzled look, "Refresh my memory and what the hell are you doing with that money? You know we all agreed to lay low for the first few weeks before we made any kind of purchases."

"Today is Saturday the 31st of January and you know what that means."

"Actually, I don't."

"It is when car dealers want to make the best end of the month deals on offloading cars from their lots. My dad always said to buy a new car on the last day of the month. And especially in the winter when cars don't move as fast. You promised we could go over to Hassett Lincoln and look at their Continental. You know I always wanted a brand-new car. I never owned one before. Besides, it's not like it's a Mercedes or BMW. The one I checked out online that is fully loaded is about forty-five thousand. We can buy it outright and keep it for the next ten years. Consider it an investment. Besides we can trade in my twelve year old Honda Accord too. I'm sure they'll give me something for it. You just have to follow me there in your car. And I'll drive slow since it is awkward for you to drive in that cast."

"Danny baby, I know you want a new car and all. But how do we explain it to our families. You know they know we don't make all that much money."

"We can tell them that we've been saving and we leased it for no money down and a zero percent interest rate. They'll buy that. Besides, I really, really, really want to go and check it out. They're open until 9pm so we have plenty of time. Just bring your car in case you want to leave. I don't want to tie up your whole afternoon. But, if you will do this for me……." She stopped talking and twirled her hair between her fingers as she walked over to him. Freddie noticed the mischievous look on her face and knew she was up to something. Danielle gave him her sexiest smile. She then reached down and slowly eased his broken foot off the ottoman. She seductively nestled herself between his legs and unzipped his pants. After reaching in and pulling out his cock, she gave Freddie the best blowjob she had in quite a while. Freddie, from pure pleasure, who was no longer able to hold off, exploded inside her mouth. Danielle took his full load in her mouth and graciously swallowed it all, ensuring herself, that Freddie was now all hers.

46

"Oh, thank you Freddie. I LOVE it! I honestly love it! I always wanted white too. I know you said white is hard to keep clean, but who cares," Danielle exclaimed as the salesmen went to finalize the paperwork.

"See I told you, people always get the best deal on the last day. And since it after six o'clock they are desperate to meet their numbers." She continued to ramble on, "Do you realize we got this car for a steal? The same as online, with the identical features was almost fifty thousand. What did we pay $37,000.00, including all taxes and motor vehicle fees."

Freddie who loved seeing his wife so excited added, "It helped that we got those two rebates. The manufacturer rebate and first time Lincoln buyer rebate. Also, since we paid for the car in cash that helped too And we traded in your old car."

"I shopped all the Lincoln dealers and believe it or not, Hassett Lincoln right here in Wantagh had the best prices."

Danielle was diligent on doing her homework for getting the best deal yet. They had driven less than four miles from their apartment on Surrey Lane in Massapequa Park to the Hassett Lincoln Dealership on Sunrise Highway. The whole experience was much more pleasurable than they anticipated. There was no real haggling back and forth on the price. Considering she was willing to pay for it in cash, made the deal go even more smoothly. The salesman had since returned and after the paperwork was finished, he told them the car would be ready in an hour or less. He then wanted to go over all the features with Danielle to ensure that she knew how all the bells and whistles worked.

As they sat in the waiting area, Danielle couldn't contain her excitement and regardless of the outcome, conferenced in both Meghan and Kimberly on her cell phone to share in her excitement. After brushing off their 'but we agreed' for the first ten minutes or so, they finally came around and saw it exactly the way she had hoped. Of the three girls, she was the least likely to ever have gotten a new car. If they hadn't come into this money, chances were slim it would ever have happened. Both Meghan and Kimberly knew this and although they weren't 100% thrilled by the sudden impulse Danielle had shown in spending the money so fast, they shrugged it off for their best friend. Just hearing the excitement in her voice, delighted them very much. So, with the promise that as soon as she drove off in her new car, she would head over to Meghan's house, she was to meet them both, so they could see her brand new car. Her first brand new car. And unfortunately, her last.

47

Danielle and Freddie were standing outside the car dealer. The salesman had just finished showing them both how to operate all the gadgets the car came with. It was close to nine o'clock and the weather was quite cold. Danielle had bundled up in her scarf and gloves, while Freddie wore a ski hat and lighter than normal jacket for this time of year. Freddie had pulled up their old car and was now parked behind their brand new car.

"I promise. Just a half hour at most. Forty-five minutes tops," pleaded Danielle.

Freddie looked at the love of his life and knew he would give in, but still wanted her to squirm and beg, "I know you and once you're with the girls, forget about it. Half an hour will turn into two hours before you know it. Besides Danny baby, I'm hungry. It felt like we were in that dealership for hours and hours."

"We were in there for hours. But I got the best deal ever. How 'bout after I visit the girls, I swing by and pick you up outside the apartment and we take my new car to 'Big Daddy's.' You love Cajun food and we haven't been there in a while. By then the restaurant won't be so packed like it always is. I will only stay long enough to show them my car and then come back. What do you say?"

"Okay, okay, it's a deal. But don't take too long. My stomach is growling from hunger, Freddie said as he rubbed his stomach and started to head back into the dealership before they closed.

Danielle noticed him turn around, "Hey, where are you going?"

"I have to use the john. I had to take a piss for the last hour. I'll just be a minute. Go visit the girls and I'll wait for you back at the house, but don't take too long. I miss you already."

48

Danielle hopped into her dream car. She blasted the heat and put the seat warmer on high. She was parked heading east to Massapequa Park and knew she had to go west toward Bellmore. She waited until the road was clear and pulled out onto Sunrise Highway. There was a turnaround right up past Massapequa Nissan and she moved over into the left lane. As she was putting on her blinker, she accidentally hit a button on her steering wheel causing the radio to turn on. The music was blasting at a volume too loud. She remembered Freddie wanting to hear just how loud the speakers cranked and they must have forgotten to lower the volume. Not fully concentrating on the road, she started to make the u-turn to head west. Her new Lincoln had just started to round the turn, but the music was so deafening that she started to fumble with all the buttons on the wheel. She was totally flustered. In the split second that she looked down again, a speeding ambulance was heading to an emergency call. An eighty-two year old woman had a heart attack and needed immediate medical assistance. The EMT driver, who was driving very fast, didn't see the car until it was too late and had no time to even swerve. He hit his brakes but to no avail. The lights and sirens should have alerted the driver of the car as they quickly approached. Danielle never even heard the sirens or saw the lights. She was too focused on turning down the volume of the radio. The ambulance hit the passenger side of Danielle's car with such force that the impact snapped her neck before she even had a chance. The side of her head slammed into the driver's side window smashing it to pieces. It all happened in a matter of seconds. The brand-new Lincoln now totaled, had been pushed up against the guardrail where it now rested. The EMT driver and his assistant weren't seriously injured thanks to the air bags that deployed upon impact. The fire truck that was in fast pursuit just seconds behind witnessed the whole thing. They immediately stopped to offer aid and radioed for another ambulance to get to the old woman who suffered a heart attack. The firemen jumped out to see what they could do. They ran over to the Lincoln first. There was no helping the driver of the car. They had seen that death stare before. They turned to help the EMT's who assured them they were okay. Just a bit banged up. Ironically, as it turned out, the old woman had survived what could have been a fatal heart attack. Unfortunately, Danielle wasn't as lucky as her luck had run out. She had died instantly at the scene.

49

Freddie had just finished his business in the men's room and was walking outside into the cold air of the late January night, when he heard sirens off in the distance. Not even a second later he heard a loud crash. He knew from the sound of it, that it was a bad accident. There was a loud screeching from tires before the collision. Then metal upon metal. He hobbled over to his car and jumped in and started his car. A couple of salesmen had followed him outside to see if they could see anything as well since they, too, had heard the accident. Freddie used his right foot still in the cast to gently step on the accelerator. He was only a few yards away, when he thought he saw a white car up against the guard rail on the other side of Sunrise Highway. His heart suddenly stopped as he got closer and knew at that precise moment, who's car it was. He sped up and stopped his car right there in the left lane. There was a fire engine with its lights flashing and a group of firefighters running back and forth from the car to what appeared to be an ambulance. He pushed open his door and wobbled over to the other side of the highway as now there were also two Nassau County Police cars there as well. One of the two cops spotted him walking toward the car and assumed he was just a nosy bystander. He rushed over to stop him, just as the firefighters were carrying over a tarp to cover the body inside the car until they could properly remove it. The scene to Freddie was so surreal. He felt like he was having an out of body experience. There was crime tape placed from the Lincoln to the ambulance. Freddie somehow made it over to the passenger side that was so pushed in that it almost touched the passenger who was driving the car. He looked in and saw Danielle's face. Her head was oddly hanging to the left. He knew her neck had been broken based on the angle. The police officer, only inches away from Freddie, came to a brisk stop when he realized that this man was anything but a gaper. He watched as Freddie fell to his knees and covered his eyes screaming out in anguish. He signaled over to the other police officer to grab a blanket, since this man was barely dressed for these frigid conditions. The other cop ran over and gave him the blanket. He placed the blanket over Freddie and let him be for the moment. His twenty-two years on the police force had told him his instincts were right. This man was related to this dead woman. The grief was written all over his face. The police officer would let Freddie come out of shock before he started to ask questions. Freddie, on the other hand, didn't feel the cold even before or after the blanket was draped over his shoulders. Freddie didn't feel a thing. His whole being was numb. He just kept crying out for his Danny baby.

50

Danielle Torres' wake was held at Clair S. Bartholomew & Son on Bedford Avenue in Bellmore, right next to Saint Barnabas Church where her funeral had taken place. Freddie, as well as Danielle's parents, were too distraught to plan her services. Freddie's mother and father, offered their guidance and support, and helped their son make the arrangements. The wake was Tuesday evening and all day Wednesday. Father Adrian McHugh, the pastor at St. Barnabas, came to the wake on Tuesday night for the prayer service. The funeral pallor had to open up an additional room to accommodate the turnout of mourners who had come to pay their respects. After Father Adrian prayed the final 'Our Father', he then asked family and friends to say a few words. Danielle's two younger brothers came forward and told stories of how their only older sister, would always be the coolest in their eyes. Each of them shared their own tales of growing up with Danielle. One could not help but notice their love for their sister and there were sobs throughout the room. The funeral owner had his assistants passing out extra tissue boxes to the overwhelmingly crying crowd. An aunt, her Godmother, made a heartfelt speech about her Goddaughter, and had most of the family and friends in tears. The aunt, herself, broke down and was inconsolable. As her husband came forward to help her back to her chair, she fainted and was caught in his arms just in time. The next day Father Adrian, with his Irish Brogue, celebrated the mass. With his salt and pepper hair and heavenly blue eyes, he stood tall behind the pulpit. His Homily engaged the whole congregation and left all the mourners in awe at his eulogy for Danielle. The Pallbearers, all members of Danielle's family including her two tearful brothers, carried her casket to the waiting hearse in front of the Church. She was to be laid to rest at St. Charles Cemetery in Farmingdale. The night before had snowed lightly and there was a dusting of fresh snow on the ground. Everyone gathered at her gravesite and watched as her coffin was lowered into the ground. The Funeral Director had roses and passed them out to each person present to place on her casket before leaving. Freddie surrounded by his own family looked gaunt and pale. He hadn't slept very well the last few nights and would wake up in the middle of the night calling out for Danielle. His older sister Cecilia stayed with him at his apartment and was the rock he now leaned on. His younger brother, Carlos, was a constant comfort to him as well. Between Cecilia and Carlos, they never left him alone. Now as the three of them walked away from his beloved one's final resting place, arm and arm with their brother, they turned to look behind to the sound of a voice calling out his name.

"Freddie, Freddie, please wait up," shouted Meghan, herself, looking grief stricken. "Kimberly and I have been trying since last night at the wake to speak with you. We are so, so, sorry. We can't even begin to……"

"Begin to what Meghan? Tell me, to what?" snapped Freddie.

Cole who had been at his wife's side, along with Matt and Kimberly trying to catch up from a few steps behind, stopped dead in their tracks from the coldness in Freddie's voice.

"We weren't even told where you were going from here. Your parents wouldn't even answer us when we asked them. What is going on? We want to be here for you. To comfort you," Meghan said in a soft voice.

Freddie stopped and pulled free from his brother and sister and walked over to the four of them. "YOU want to comfort me?," he laughed out loud. "Ha, really! Danielle could comfort me. My sister and brother here can comfort me. Even my mom and pops could comfort me. Not you though. Any of you. You fucking guys are NO comfort to me. Never really were. If it weren't for you bitches….."

Matt took a step closer to Freddie but Cole pulled him back. Realizing that it was Freddie lashing out in grief, Matt let him continue by just saying, "That's no way to speak about our wives. I know your grieving but don't make a scene."

The crowd of mourners had also stopped to watch this exchange unfold. Even Danielle's parents and two siblings were speechless and just stood there silently listening to Freddie's outburst.

Freddie couldn't hold back, as he raised his voice, and lashed out some more, "Or what Matt? You gonna punch me in the nose again. Just try it. I'll fucking knock you out! And as for your WIVES. Is that better? If it weren't for them telling Danielle to come show them her car, she would have fucking came straight the hell home. But NOOO........,"

Both, Meghan and Kimberly gasped at his last statement. Kimberly couldn't contain herself now and also felt her voice rising, "Really, IS that what YOU fucking think Freddie? Danielle wanted to show US and asked US to be there for HER. You see, we too, were always there for HER. We lost OUR best friend also. And this is how you treat us. By ignoring us since the first night of the wake. We all knew something was up since you made it so obvious. But you know what? We consider you a friend and let you mourn without us. Apparently that's what you wanted. But by blaming us for her death, shame on you Freddie. It was an accident. Plain and simple. A fucking accident." Kimberly starting crying and put her head in Matt's chest.

Freddie who didn't care one way or another for these so-called friends decided what next needed to be said to make his last point hit home to these two couples. He knew by saying this, their friendship with him would be over once and for all, but Freddie didn't care at this point. The true link to these people was Danielle and she was no longer there. So with bated breath he continued, "You see, I never really gave a rat's ass about any of you. I did it for my Danny baby. You four are nothing to me. You never meant anything to me. Not now, not ever. As far as I'm concerned, you can all rot in hell. So get outta my fucking face and spend your money wisely. Or better yet, as Danielle did, spend it poorly. So, FUCK off!"

Meghan felt her knees start to buckle as she took hold of Cole to steady herself on her feet. She couldn't believe what she was hearing spew from Freddie's mouth. Kimberly looked over at Freddie in total shock as Matt clenched his fists ready to attack.

Carlos had heard enough from his brother and pulled Freddie's arm and whisked him away in the other direction, knowing that if he didn't at that moment, all hell would break loose. If only he knew that hell hath no fury and was breaking loose very shortly.

51

Over the course of the next two weeks, Meghan, Cole, Kimberly and Matt spent as much time together as possible. Both girls took a full week off from their jobs to mourn the loss of their best friend properly. Meghan and Kimberly talked about Danielle as if she were still alive. They would reminisce about their past over and over. So much so, that Cole and Matt could repeat the stories verbatim. When Valentine's day came, the girls had purchased a cemetery blanket of roses and went to place it on Danielle's grave. The pile of dirt was still in a mound, since it had not been that long since they buried her. Luckily for them, Freddie was nowhere in sight, however it did look like he was recently there, since a box of Chocolates were left there too.

52

It was now nearing the end of February and time still hadn't healed the girl's wounds. It would take years for them to overcome their loss. They went about their daily business as usual and called each other two to three times a day for reassurance.

"So, tell me where are you guys looking to buy?" Meghan inquired.

Kimberly with excitement in her voice answered, "Point Lookout. Three houses in from the beach on Lynbrook Avenue. Matt can just run into the ocean and catch all the waves he wants. And it was a foreclosure as well. We're heading over there right after breakfast to make the real estate agent an official offer. So far, we outbid the other three offers. Can you believe it? I always wanted a house close to the beach. We can just stroll on down on a hot summer day and there we are. If we put a binder on it, I'll have to take you and Dan......." The tone of her voice went from happy to sad in a brief second.

"That's okay sweetie. I do that all the time too. So much so, I have to catch myself at least once or twice a day. It still feels so surreal. Like she'll walk through my door at any second, bitching about something."

'Yes, she was good about bitching. But always in a Danielle friendly bitching way."

Both girls laughed as they once again remembered their best friend.

"I gotta scoot. We have to be there by 1pm and then Matt's taking me out to a fancy schmancy seaford restaurant in Bayshore. You guys should join us if you're free."

"Wish we could, but we have Cole's Uncle's 65th surprise birthday party at 7pm. Besides, we're supposed to be getting some more snow later this afternoon. Not much but it could be an inch or two. So, be careful. And love ya Kimberly."

"Love you way the heck more Meghan. Catch up with you tomorrow on Sunday after church."

"Sounds like a plan."

Little did they know their plans were about to change.

53

Matt snuck up on his Aunt Mary, who was sitting at their kitchen table, playing her usual games on her I-pad. She loved playing 'Candy Crush' and the 'Wizard of Oz' slots.

"How's my favorite Aunt doing?," Matt said as he leaned over and kissed her on the cheek. "Kim and I are heading out to put a binder on that house I told you about. You're going to love it. You will have to spend some weekends in the summer out by us. We will set up a guest bedroom just for you. I'm just waiting for Kimberly to finish up in the bathroom and we're driving over to meet with the real estate agent at 1pm. After, I'm taking her to Fatfish on the water in Bayshore. I heard they have excellent lobster specials. Don't know what time we'll be back. I want to surprise Kim with the……."

"Surprise me with what?," Kimberly asked. "There's only three restaurants in Bayshore on the water. Captain Bill's, Fatfish or Nicky's clam bar. I googled them on my phone. I'm hoping Fatfish since I've been wanting to go there for so long."

"Must you always spoil the fun. Can't I ever surprise you? And speaking of surprises, I was waiting for Kimberly before I gave this to you." Matt went over to the kitchen counter and took the brown lunch bag off it and walked over to his Aunt. "I know with us buying a new home and all you are probably worried about how you're going to pay the property taxes. Kimberly and I want to give you a little something that should cover at least two years or more of them. You've been so good to me after all these years, it's the least we can do. You know we discussed you selling this house, but darn it you can be so stubborn. I know you've been here your whole life, but we have two extra bedrooms. You should just move in with us."

Aunt Mary Quigley was seventy-seven years old. She was a plump old woman with thin white hair and a face full of wrinkles from years spent down by the ocean over the summers. Her eyes were a grayish green and still full of life. She took the bag and peeked in asking, "Are these all hundred dollar bills? Where by the love of God, did you come across this kind of money? And just how much did you give me?"

Kimberly and Matt smiled with the satisfaction that they were doing the right thing. They both knew that Aunt Mary would be lonely without them, but deep down she wanted them to own their own home. They also surmised that in three years at most, she would be living with them. They would let her stay in the house just long enough to realize that she needed to be with them. Soon enough she would come to her senses and once again they would be reunited.

"Twenty-five thousand to be exact," Matt said saving her from having to count it herself.

Aunt Mary looked up at them, "Did you say twenty-five thousand? I can't accept this. Have you two gone crazy? After all, you two are buying your first home yourselves."

"Don't worry about this money or where it came from. It's the least we can do after all you've done for us. Besides, didn't you always teach me to just say thank you when someone gives you a present or a gift," Matt stated.

Aunt Mary had taught her nephew well and couldn't argue his point. Instead she replied, "Come here you two and give your Aunt a great big hug. If you both insist, then hot dog, I won't look a gift horse in the mouth. Besides, that's too much to keep in the house until Monday. I think Chase Bank in the Village is open until two o'clock on Saturdays. I'll just take a quick shower and head over and deposit this. I'm too nervous with this kind of money laying around. I'll feel safer if I do this. Besides, if you don't mind, I might use a thousand or so right off the bat. Money has been tight lately and I didn't want to trouble you two. I've been meaning to call PSEG, our local gas company, to check out the boiler downstairs. Is it me or do you both ever smell a faint order of gas?"

Both Matt or Kimberly shook their heads in disagreement of smelling any unusual odors of gas. They were too overjoyed with the prospect of purchasing their own first home. The possibility of a gas leak was the furthest thing on their minds. Perhaps it should have been a priority.

54

As Aunt Mary climbed the stairs up to her bedroom on the second floor, she heard Matt and Kimberly shout their goodbyes once again. My how she adored and loved them both so much. It was a little after noon and she really wanted to make the bank before they closed. She headed into the master bath off her bedroom and quickly undressed out of her nightgown and robe and jumped in the shower. She put the hot water as high up as her body would allow. She hated taking a cold shower and never understood how other people did. Aunt Mary was never truly fond of the cold and winter months. Even more so as she got older. Aunt Mary had started to dread the winters as they approached each year. Recently over the last decade or so there were too many snowstorms one after the other. Storms that dropped heavy accumulations of snow that came with them. She was grateful, however, for her nephew whenever there was a snowstorm or blizzard. He was always up and out before she even made a mention as to the shoveling being done. Knowing Matt, even with his own home, he would still come over and dig her out. The days where neighborhood boys would come around and ask if you wanted your walkway shoveled were long gone. And the ones that did offer wanted to charge you an arm and leg to do it. She lathered up her body rather quickly, shampooed her hair and rinsed off. She put on a jogging suit that she had from the seventies and still fit in and didn't bother to blow dry her hair. She was only going outside and straight in her car. No need to waste another twenty minutes or more drying and setting her hair and taking the chance the bank would close before she got there. She knew leaving with a wet head was not a smart idea. Just how bad an idea, she would soon find out.

55

The first thing Aunt Mary noticed as she took out her winter coat from the closet was that it had started to snow. The weatherman had predicted it would snow later in the afternoon, closer to dinner time. So much for accurate weather forecasts. She laughed to herself that even she at her age could do a better job as a weatherperson. Now, as she peered out the bay window in her living room, she saw snowflakes coming down that looked to be the size of quarters. Already they were sticking to the ground. She put the paper bag of money in her larger than normal pocketbook. Kimberly had given her at least four or five smaller ones for either her birthday or Christmas over the years, but she always chose her own. She had gotten it long ago at Green Acres Mall in Valley Stream at a store named Korvettes, which no longer existed. That's how old her bag was. She paid $14.99 for it and that was a fortune back in the day. Aunt Mary sure got her money's worth from this handbag. As she donned her gloves and scarf, she put a hat over her still damp hair. She tried to towel dry it, but it was still very wet. There was no time to stop and think about that now. With the snow coming down at a steady pace, she would need to drive more slowly on the roads. She opened the front door and made her way down the walk to the driveway where her car was parked. She hit the door button on her remote and was just about to open the door handle when she heard an animal cry out. It sounded like it was coming from her backyard. Aunt Mary was an animal lover and although she hadn't owned a pet in several years, she still had a soft spot for other people's pets. Again, she heard the soft cry of an animal in distress. It sounded like the Hymans cat next door. They had mentioned to Aunt Mary just this past Thursday that they were leaving at the crack of dawn to drive upstate. She remembered they had said it was this coming Saturday. Aunt Mary glanced next door and noticed their SUV wasn't parked in its usual spot in the driveway. She assumed Glenn and Debbie Hyman had already left early this morning to visit their daughter, who attended college up in Syracuse. It was their daughter's birthday weekend and she had asked them to come up. Again, she heard the wail of what she now was certain to be a cat. Aunt Mary went over to the six foot tall white PVC fence and opened the latch to let herself into her yard. She immediately took notice of just how fast the snow was coming down. At this rate their prediction of just an inch or two was going to be way off target. She worried that Matt and Kimberly might get stuck in it. The cat was mewing even louder as she got closer. Aunt Mary couldn't quite see where the cat was and wasn't even sure if it even belonged to the Hyman's. Whatever the case may be, one way or another she would let the cat in her house until the snow had stopped. Aunt Mary heard the cat crying, but couldn't figure out from which direction the sound was coming. She made her way onto the cement patio and was walking toward the back steps to go through the house rather than face the chill of the cold air that she hated. The cat was up in the only tree in the yard. It was a stray that a couple of the neighbors felt bad for and fed. Aunt Mary couldn't quite pinpoint it's location or where the sound was coming from. Then she heard it again and knew where it must be; in her willow tree. She had started to twirl around to face the cat, when out of the blue, it leapt off the branch it was resting on, and landed by her feet. Aunt Mary was so startled that she lost her footing and stumbled backwards. And as her hand released her much cherished pocketbook, it went flying up and off in the wind. Aunt Mary tried desperately to catch her balance but couldn't. She fell backwards and landed smack on her back, hitting her head on the back brick stoop. She cracked her skull open and the blood was already gushing out. Frantically she reached her hand back and took hold of her still wet dripping hair. She didn't know if it was the water she had felt or the blood. Either way she knew she needed help fast. Aunt Mary tried to move but the excruciating pain radiating from her back, caused her to scream out. She must have broken her back. She rolled over onto her side and watched as the blood came flowing past her face. She immediately saw this and vomited. The Mafucci's, her next-door neighbors on the other side of her house, had left on Wednesday for a wrestling tournament. Their son had placed second from his high school for the district and was asked to compete up in Albany at the All-State wrestling conference. They were not at home either. She felt her body weakening from the loss of blood. Her hair felt as if it were frozen and sticking to her head. She rolled over onto her back again. Aunt Mary started shivering from the cold and tried to wrap her arms around her body. She knew no one was around to save her as she gazed up into the heavens. Her voice was too frail and weak at this point to holler for help. Aunt Mary's once vibrant gray-green eyes had started to glaze over as her life was slipping away. She started to pray the prayer she said over and over from when she was a small child. In a very soft voice, racked with pain, she said, "Hail Mary full of Grace. The lord is with thee….."as she took in her last breath, but never continued, and closed her eyes forever.

Sadly enough, it would be hours before Matt and Kimberly would eventually arrive home to find her dead in the backyard. By then, her body would be frozen solid under the eight inches of snow, also surrounded by a pool of bright red frozen blood.

56

March had come in like a lion with another two snowstorms, not as bad as the previous few, and went out like a lamb. Aunt Mary Quigley had a one day wake service and a funeral mass at Our Lady of Grace Roman Catholic Church in West Babylon. As her will stated, she was to be cremated and her ashes spread out along Gilgo beach. This is where she spent many hours watching Matt surf as a teenager into adulthood. Matt obeyed her wishes and after buying an urn to place some of her ashes in for a keepsake, he along with Kimberly, Meghan and Cole, went down to the beach the first spring like day in early April, and let the cool breeze take her ashes away and out to sea. Meghan and Cole kept themselves available and spent much of their free time with their two closest friends over these last few weeks.

The sun was shining brightly and the afternoon

temperature was nearing sixty. As they were walking back to Cole's Yukon, Matt was still distraught from the loss of his second mom asked no one in particular, "Why? I mean how? If only we would have waited for her to leave first."

Kimberly, who felt the loss just as deeply, took his hand in hers and replied, "Matt, you have to stop beating yourself up over this. All the coulda's, woulda's, shoulda's, isn't ever going to bring Aunt Mary back. I know it's been only six weeks since the accident, but it's going to take you time to grieve her. Look at Meghan and I and even you guys for that matter. We still can't get past Danielle. And now this. Life sucks. It really does!" Kimberly reached into her bag and pulled out a pack of cigarettes and lit one.

Meghan looked on in surprise as Kimberly did this and asked, "And when did you start smoking again. I thought you gave up that habit over ten years ago. Remember how bad it was to kick it then. Why go through that all over again? You, yourself, said it was disgusting. That your own mouth felt like an ashtray."

Kimberly took a long puff on the bud and exhaled, "With all this shit happening, I needed something to calm my nerves. It's not like I'm smoking one after the other. I bought this pack last week and I only smoked seven. And to top it off, we had to renege from the Point Lookout house. Too much happened and the thought of selling Aunt Mary's house right now. The timing isn't right. We can always look again down the line. It's not like we're going anywhere. If only there were those guarantees in life.

57

Matt watched as Kimberly got out of bed, ate her breakfast, dressed for work and left. His head was still not right. He missed his Aunt Mary more than words could ever express. Even though he lost both his parents to cancer so close apart, this loss was different. Perhaps it was due to the fact, that he was just a teenager when they passed. He was more concerned about his friends and all the extra attention he was getting, rather than losing his mother and father for good. With Kimberly's permission, since they discussed all their financial decisions, he had given up his bartending shifts for the last seven weeks at the two establishments he worked for. Plus, with over five hundred thousand, money really wasn't an issue. Both of his employers were sympathetic and assured him that his jobs were still available to him when he desired to come back. The customers loved his friendly personality and he was also a great mixologist. Matt shuffled his feet as he rose out of bed. It was April 8th and the forecast called for a record low of forty-five. Just last week two days after they laid Aunt Mary's ashes out to sea, there was a record high of seventy-five. These weather patterns were so inconsistent. Before Matt knew it, summer would be here enabling to surf everyday. He threw on his bathing trunks and walked down to the kitchen and took out the orange juice. He poured himself a large glass. He then took his daily men's multi vitamin, along with a B-12 and children's aspirin for his heart and swallowed the pills down with the OJ. He still didn't feel 100%. Perhaps if he went down to Gilgo beach, he may be able to catch some early morning waves. For this time of year, the water was still cold, which kept many surfers away. In addition, colder than normal temperatures, the surf would probably be all his. At this point, Matt longed for the seclusion. Over the years, he had made many friends surfing, but today he was looking forward to complete isolation. He went back up to his bedroom and brushed his teeth and put on some layers of clothes. He went down to the basement and grabbed his wetsuit and surf board. As he was coming up the steps, he stopped at the top landing. His nose caught a whiff of something that smelled like rotten eggs. Matt knew he read somewhere what a rotten egg smell was. He told himself that when he got back from surfing he would go online and see what it meant. Right now though, his head needed to be cleared from all the pain he was suffering. Unbeknownst to him, it was only just beginning.

58

Matt couldn't believe the morning he was having. Gilgo beach was deserted and he had the whole ocean to himself. He was amped up. The waves were perfect. According to the Weather Channel on his phone, heavy rain was expected overnight and there was a storm brewing out in the ocean. A couple of times he had to 'bail', which is when you jump off your board to avoid an imminent wipeout. Once or twice he did 'eat it' and wiped out on a wave. Matt tried to stay away from the 'impact zone', where the waves broke. He laid flat on his stomach on his surfboard and paddled out using each arm as an oar. The wetsuit he wore was insulated since the water temperature was extremely cold. And with all the energy he could muster, he was very warm wearing it. Once he felt he was far enough out, he waited as wave after wave caught his board and he rode them in. Matt hadn't felt this exhilarated in quite some time. All he thought about was his timing of his board to the waves. At this point, nothing else mattered. He was totally free of any grief, despair or anguish. It was him against the sea. Ever since he had turned fifteen and upon his Aunt Mary's insistence, he loved to surf. It was just him, his board, and the onrushing waves. Riding the crest of a wave was like being on top of the world. Matt didn't know exactly how long he had been out. The water was getting choppy now. He figured he had maybe another six rides left in him to catch, before calling it a day. Matt looked up into the sky. He had to shield his eyes, as the bright sun was blinding. He didn't care as he felt better than he had in the last two months. So good in fact, since not only from his Aunt Mary's passing, but also from the loss of Danielle, that he truly believed that he was going to be okay in the long run. Deep down, he would always think of them and miss them. As it was now, a day didn't go by that he didn't remember something his aunt said or did. He even missed Danielle's bitchy attitude. The same could not be said when it came Danielle's husband, Freddie Torres. Matt didn't really care one way or another about Freddie, whom they hadn't seen since the episode at Danielle's grave. Freddie made it a point to disappear from their lives. Frankly, Matt thought Freddie was a dick. No, Matt reconsidered and thought more of an asshole.

59

Matt had been riding in the swells caused by the approaching storm out in the ocean. Wave after breaking wave had Matt barely taking time to catch his breath. He felt like he was a teenager again. Not giving himself enough time to recuperate after each ride in, he was back on his stomach paddling out for the next big one to come. It was more than an hour later and he was way past his allotted six or seven that he had told himself before. Matt, paddled out quite a distance, sat up on his board, just as he saw a rarity in these parts of the ocean. What appeared to be a plunging breaker was fast approaching. Matt jumped up on his feet. He knew this was going to be a high crest to ride in. He was probably going to make this his last. Suddenly, and for no apparent reason, something told him to look down. It was then that he realized, he never fastened the Velcro strap from his board to his ankle. In all his years of surfing, Matt could count on one hand just how many times he hadn't done this. Now, of all the times to forget, he had seconds to prepare himself for the fast-approaching break. He knew now that if he panicked, it would do him no good. The huge wave hit the back of his board and brought him high up on the crest. Matt was riding it in at top speed, when suddenly the wave came crashing down faster than expected. Matt was flung off the board and into the rushing water. He lost his bearings as he tried in vain to get his head out from under the twisting churning water current. His body was pulled under once again. Matt, having been a lifeguard as well, let the current subside for a moment, and with lightning speed, he sprung up until his head broke the surface. He had swallowed some water and the first thing he did was spit it out. He then took in a large gulp of air. Matt treaded water, until he felt like he had control of the situation. Matt's head bobbed in the water as he tried to get his bearings as to which direction the shoreline was. He tried to use his one hand to block the reflection of the sun on the water. It temporarily blinded him. Another wave about the same size as the last crashed just yards in front of him. With it came his surfboard, as it rose up and out of the water. Matt had forgotten it wasn't attached to him. Without a moment to react, or even a second to throw his arms up, the board lifted into the air, and came crashing down into his forehead with such force, it knocked him unconscious. Matt's head gently went back below the surface. The constant waves would eventually wash his body up on the shoreline. It would be found just a half hour later by a young couple walking their dog on the beach. A gruesome discovery on such a clear bright day. The police would arrive shortly afterwards and find his identification in his backpack up on the sand near his clothes. The call would be made to a Mrs. Kimberly Quigley to come to Good Samaritan Hospital in West Islip to identify the body of her husband. And as for Matt Quigley, his family tree would never branch out again.

60

Meghan Maercker had requested an FML (family medical leave) from her job as an Administrative Assistant at Cold Spring Hills. Her boss as well as her friend for the past six years, Marybeth, had felt sorry for the unimaginable deaths that had taken place over the last few months. She actually insisted Meghan take time off to be with Kimberly, who was in a state of shock herself. It had been less than a week since Matt's body washed up on shore and Meghan and Cole were helping their friend make the arrangements. Matt had no other family other than his Aunt Mary, who had died an unfortunate death less than two months before. Kimberly opted to cremate Matt and to scatter his ashes at the same beach where his Aunt Mary's remains had been spread. She felt by doing this, Matt and his Aunt would spend eternity floating together as one on the beach that brought them such fond memories over the years. At Cole's request Kimberly was staying with them. Kimberly's mother lived in Bellmore and wanted her to stay with her and her new husband. Her parents had divorced when she was three, and her father moved out west to Fort Collins in Colorado. Both her parents remarried, but only her mother chose to have another baby. Her younger brother, Tyler, had just turned thirteen and was giving his parents a run for their money. He had gotten in with a rowdy crowd and was grounded more times than not these last few months. From the stories her mom had shared regarding Tyler, if they didn't get a handle on him rather quickly, he was heading in the wrong direction. Kimberly didn't need to be around a troubled teenager at this point, so she refused her mother's offer. The lawyers who owned the law firm in Garden City gave her an indefinite leave, telling her that her position would always be there for her if she ever wanted to return. They, too, had noticed that she began smoking and weren't in the practice of hiring paralegals who did. In a way, they had hoped she would take all the time in the world she needed to deal with her loss. They never imagined that in the future, she would never come back.

61

"Leave me the fuck alone will you. Why all the questions?," Kimberly slurred. "It's like the third fucking degree with you lately. My own mom would question me less." She reached over and poured some more Dewar's Scotch Whiskey into the rocks glass and chugged it down in one gulp.

Meghan was furious as she walked over to Kimberly who was seated on their couch and grabbed the bottle from her hands, "Bad enough you went from one or two cigarettes a day up to what is it now? Almost two packs a day."

"I got a lot on my mind in case you forget, I mean forgot," Kimberly said sounding more and more tipsy by the minute. "After all….," She threw her hands up in the air. "I did just lose my husband and his Aunt. Not to mention one of my two closest friends. So…..please….. pretty please……………give me back my bottle."

Cole stood in the doorway listening to this whole scene play out. As much as he felt Kimberly's pain, she, too, was heading down a path of destruction. First the smoking and now not just drinking, but heavily drinking until she gotten so drunk, that she passed out. As much as he wanted to put in his two cents in the matter, he left it up to his wife to steer her back on track.

"Listen to me Kimberly. I can't explain what the hell is going on and why these tragedies are all happening one after the other either. But I need you to face them head on. Drinking yourself to death……..," Meghan covered her mouth, trying to take back the words. "Oh God, I didn't mean that. Not that word for sure."

"Mean what? Say it Meghan. Drinking myself to death will what? Kill me. As if losing my husband won't."

"I didn't mean it like that and you know it. I'm just really worried and concerned for you. If anything were to happen to you like it did Danielle, I wouldn't be able to cope. Please just reconsider what I'm asking. Lay off the bottle and cut back on the cigarettes and cry on MY shoulder if you want. All I'm asking is that I want the old Kimberly back. I'm afraid of this one."

"Frightened of me because I have a drink or two to drown out my sorrows. Shame on you!"

"Please, Kimberly. I do this because I LOVE you. I'm not trying to bombard you with any sort of demands. I'm just pleading with you to kick back a bit on the bottle and ease up with the smoking. If not for me, then for yourself."

Kimberly looked at her best friend and knew she may be right but wouldn't let her know it. She also decided at that moment that she would no longer drink in front of Meghan or Cole, who had been watching the whole thing, from the hallway leading into the living room. Kimberly would stash the liquor at her house in West Babylon and consume it there, where she wouldn't be judged. This way she wouldn't offend anyone.

Meghan was still rambling on about their friendship, but all Kimberly was hearing right now was 'blah, blah, blah'. Meghan's voice was getting on her nerves.

Deciding she had heard enough, Kimberly was ready to call it a night, she tried to lift herself off of the couch but tumbled back down giggling as she did, "Oopsie, Cole can you give this girl a hand. Or a foot. I seem to have fallen and I can't get up. I do believe, I need to sleep this whole thing off."

Cole went over to Kimberly and with two hands pulled her to her feet. Meghan took hold of her from her side and led her into their guest bedroom. The bedroom that was to eventually become the baby's room if, indeed, Meghan was ever to become pregnant. They had been trying for years now, and Meghan felt like time was running out. But as the clock was ticking, and time would have it, the day was drawing near.

62

Meghan had been pacing back and forth for most of the afternoon. It was April 15th, income tax due date, and Cole had some unfinished business at the law firm he worked at. Usually he was home by seven and it was fast approaching eight. He texted her that he was on his way home. She had hoped he would get home before Kimberly to share the news. Kimberly's mom had picked her up at seven and took her and her brother, Tyler, out to dinner at Outback in Merrick, to try to cheer her daughter up. The Outback was running their occasional special for their steak and lobster tail, which was Kimberly's favorite. Meghan had prepared Cole's all-time favorite dish as well. She had set the table and took the food out of the oven and placed the dish in the center. Everything looked perfect. Without a minute to spare, Meghan heard a car pull into the driveway. Standing in the living room, she went over and moved the curtains to peek out the window. The driver of the Yukon shut off the engine. Cole stepped out, and headed towards the front door. Meghan clapped her hands together, mostly from the exciting news she was about to share with her husband. She quickly opened the door just as Cole was about to place his hand on it. Startled he said, "Whoa, when was the last time you ever opened the front door for me?" He stepped into the living room and scratched his chin. "Hmm……Lets see. If my memory serves me correctly. Never."

Meghan was elated and was beaming from cheek to cheek. She grabbed hold of him and wrapped her arms around his neck, "Smart aleck. Give me a kiss you great big fool." She stood on her tippy toes and planted a kiss on his lips.

"And what may I ask is that delicious aroma wafting through the house?"

Meghan was pulling him into the dining room where she had set their best china and silverware. There was a bottle of apple cider and two champagne glasses. There was also a Heineken Light beer next to a frosted mug next to his plate. "I made you your favorite. Chicken cutlet parmigian with spaghetti. Now, sit, sit. No wait, better yet stand still." Meghan was acting like a schoolgirl, which had Cole smiling at her behavior. Instead of getting right to the point, Meghan went into the whole scenario, "With all that's been happening to us and all the grief, the last thing I should be is smiling or happier than I have been in months. Regardless, either way I haven't been thinking about us, or trying for a baby in case you haven't noticed."

Cole, himself, was consumed with dealing with these

deaths as well and on top of it all, performing his daily duties as a lawyer. His stress level was at an all-time high and he wondered how he hadn't had a heart attack himself.

Meghan continued, "Well, like I said. One month led into the next and I lost track of my periods. I went to see Dr. Ferrari for my routine exam. And guess what she told me?" Meghan's pitch in her voice rose a decibel as she blurted out, "We're having a BABY! A baby, Cole! I'm already out of my first trimester."

Cole stuck a finger in his ear and asked, "Did I hear what I think I heard? We.....I mean us.....How? When? Where?......" His voice just got higher too.

"Slow down slugger." Meghan laughed. "First off, you know the how. The when and the where if I'm to guess was up at the cabin. When we practically ripped each other's clothes off. I backtracked and it had to be that weekend. With all that has happened since, our lovemaking hasn't been a priority. Dr. Ferrari told me that my due date is October 9th."

"This coming October. Wow so close. I told you it would happen. So, it took us a bit longer than we hoped. But God dang it. It finally happened. I can't tell you how happy this makes me. Us! We're going to be parents. A mommy and daddy. This calls for a celebration." Cole looked over at the table and knew Meghan was one step ahead of him. "I say we toast to the newest Maercker." He lifted the apple cider and started to pour Meghan a glass. He then poured himself one and raised his to clink with hers as he toasted, "Here's to our future. May it look brighter than it has. A new Maercs to the clan. And I know you'll be a great mommy. And to me a great daddy!"

What he didn't know was that the future looked only bleak.

63

The next few months were uneventful as Meghan and Cole counted the weeks until their new arrival. She was nearly six months pregnant. Meghan still hadn't gone back to work and with Cole's insistence had been dipping into their found money lately to subsidize her loss of income. Marybeth, her Director at the Adult Day Care, granted her a temporary leave of absence, knowing fully well her dearest friend wouldn't be returning anytime soon. Kimberly had since moved back to her house in West Babylon and she, too, had not gone back to work either. Meghan was certain Kimberly still drank but kept it hidden from her the best she could. Whenever they were together, Kimberly either chewed gum or popped Altoids in her mouth one after the other. She couldn't hide the fact she was still smoking. Although, she sprayed perfume over her clothes to cover the smell, Meghan knew better and surmised she still hadn't kicked the habit. Either way, Meghan was not going there today. They met halfway for lunch at Mercato Kitchen and Cocktails in Massapequa. Both hadn't stepped foot in the gym for months and felt guilty for their lack of exercise, so they ordered a chicken Caesar salad to split and two iced teas.

Kimberly looking like she was coming off a hangover took a bite of her salad while asking, "So when do you find out the sex? And what about names? The names choices seem endless and so cool too." She took a big sip of the water on the table. "I'm so happy for you both. You are BOTH going to be great parents."

Meghan put down the glass of iced tea she had just finished drinking and answered her, "We could have found out the sex about two months ago, but Cole is old fashioned that way and doesn't want to know. Kinda wants it to be a surprise. I'm okay with that. Although it feels like time is crawling at this point, we already waited this long. What's three more months. And as far as names. We haven't talked about it, but Cole and I are going out tomorrow for dinner. We haven't done that in such a long time. I'm hoping to bounce some names off of him and see what he thinks. We're trying that new Italian Restaurant in Bellmore on the corner of Merrick Road. I forgot the name. I feel like it changes owners every time I pass it. Right now, it's called Molto Bene. I heard the food and service were excellent."

"Nice. Well let me know what names you settle on for either a boy or girl. Matt loves the name Ava Rose. Said that would be the name if we had a girl. And Liam for a boy. As if I had no choice in the picking. He cracks me up................" Kimberly realized she was talking as if he were still alive. She picked up her napkin off her lap and dabbed at her eye that started to tear. Meghan felt for her friend and didn't utter a word. She just placed her hand over Kimberly's, as they sat there in silence. Meghan thinking what a shame it was for Kimberly losing Matt and Kimberly's only thought was, she couldn't wait to get home and have a couple of drinks.

64

"We'll take your best champagne. I see you have the 2004 Dom Perignon Rose Limited Edition. One of those please." The waiter smiled and shook his head yes as he scooted away to get a bottle that was sure to boost the check ensuring him a hefty tip.

It was a Wednesday night in mid-July and Meghan made an eight o'clock reservation at the restaurant Molto Bene, the one she had mentioned to Kimberly over lunch. It was a very low key quaint Italian eatery. On this particular night, the restaurant was empty except for an elderly couple sitting across the restaurant from them. It looked as if there was just the one waiter who filled in as bartender and busboy. There were so many eateries along Merrick Road which made it all the more difficult for restaurants to survive. Perhaps that is why this establishment kept changing it's name over the years.

Pushing that thought aside, Meghan took her finger and worked it down the wine list until it rested on the champagne he just requested. "Are you for real. $499.00 dollars for one bottle?"

"Nothing too good for my missus."

"You do know I can't drink alcohol. I'm carrying your little, what do you call the baby......Maercs"

Cole held up his phone and showed her his screen, "I figured you would put up a fight. I did a bit of research just in case. And well according to MD on google, one cocktail in your second trimester is not going to do any damage to the little one. And right here it says a glass or two of champagne is equivalent to a glass of red wine. I promise

I won't force you to drink after this. I want only the best for you. One glass and if that is too much, I'll polish off the rest." He laughed. "We need this. Besides we haven't celebrated anything in quite some time. We've been through so much. Tonight, there is no turning back. The sky's the limit." He leaned over and whispered, "And truthfully we haven't even put a dent in that money of ours. I took two thousand with me and I plan on spending the whole thing."

Meghan shook her head in disbelief, "I can't believe you. You amaze me Mr. Cole. At the rate you're going with a $500.00 hundred dollar bottle of champagne, that shouldn't be too hard."

They had just finished splitting a Caesar Salad and their next course was to split an order of mussels in a white clam sauce. They passed on the linguini as they didn't want to fill up before the main course. For their dinner entrée Cole ordered his all-time favorite fish dish, Lobster Fra Diavolo, and Meghan ordered the Filet Mignon in a mushroom gravy.

The waiter had poured Cole another glass of Dom Perignon and went to pour Meghan another but she politely placed her hand over the rim. She knew her limit regardless of what the google doctor might say. She really didn't want one but didn't want to disappoint Cole and the festive mood he was in. She knew he had been under a great deal of pressure lately and the fact that Kimberly had stayed with them for a while to get her past her depression added to his stress. The least she could do was share in his happiness, even if it meant one measly glass.

The more than attentive waiter served them the mussels by clearing the middle of the cozy table and placing them in the center. He put a bowl next to each of them for the shells.

Cole dug in and sucked out his first, then second, followed by a third mussel before she even took one.

Rather than try to keep up with Cole, Meghan stared over at her husband and couldn't believe how lucky she was. She saw how women took a double take whenever they saw him. His light blue eyes caught most people's attention and he was quite often paid compliments about them. He stood over six feet tall and towered over many men but never made them feel small. He was the whole package and Meghan hoped that whatever sex their baby was, that they would have his looks and personality. One to die for.

A rather unusual cough escaped Cole's throat. Meghan had never heard him cough quite like that over the years, but paid no real attention at first. He was busily throwing out ridiculous baby names to get her goat.

"I got them. You'll love these. Mildred and Harold. Final answer."

Meghan wiped her fingers off on her napkin. She started to reach in to grab another mussel. "Really, that's the best you got." Playing along she offered up, "I like those two, but I was thinking more along the lines of Cleopatra and Julius."

Cole, who had since started to sweat, picked up his napkin and wiped his brow, "I like those. Better still how about Tarzan or Jane? No seriously, what names do you like or have in mind?" He took a sip of the ice water on the table and asked, "Is it me or is it hot in here all of a sudden?" He pulled at his shirt that was now clinging to him.

The room temperature was bit on the colder side, which left Meghan feeling chilly. She was wondering just how her husband could have been sweating. It was the middle of July and she was certain they had the air conditioner on.

Cole was now dripping from perspiration. He suddenly looked very out of place and once again, he had a coughing fit that was one like she never seen before. As soon as Cole stopped his eyes started to bulge out a bit. His neck was exposed, since he was wearing a V-neck argyle sweater, and a sudden outburst of hives also appeared. Cole tried to say something but no words came out. He pushed back in his chair alerting the waiter, who ran over to see what was happening. He grasped at his throat and was gasping for air. Meghan jumped up and screamed for somebody to do something, anything. The elderly couple sat there and offered no assistance. Not because they didn't want to, but they didn't know what else to do. The young waiter ran over to the bar and picked up the phone, screaming for 911 to get an ambulance here and fast. Meghan pleaded with Cole to relax and take a deep breath, which she knew was useless. Cole opened his mouth as Meghan ran over and pulled his lips apart. His tongue was so swollen, she couldn't see the back of his throat. He was staggering like he was drunk. The chef, a Spanish middle aged man, appeared from the kitchen, but he too, was useless. Five people and no one knew how to help, as Cole's face now turned blue. Cole was trying desperately to catch his breath. He didn't know what was happening to him. All he did know was that no air was getting into his lungs. If he didn't get oxygen soon, he surly would die. Cole didn't want to die. He wanted to be there to be his child's father. No, he wanted to be his or her dad. To teach them to ride a bike, swim, ski, and everything a dad would do for his child. To protect them from harm or for getting in harm's way. To love them like there was no tomorrow. With his last effort, he looked over at Meghan, whom he had always thought he would grow old with, and now knew would never take place. Meghan looked on in horror as his last few steps had him tumbling over a tabletop and falling to the floor. What was supposed to be a night of celebration, would now be forever known as a tragic event. Her husband, her lover and her best friend was going to die right before her eyes, and there was nothing she could do to stop it. She would blame herself forever. Meghan would also later learn, after the ambulance arrived and found him dead on the restaurant floor, that he went into Anaphylactic shock from the mussels. There would be no rhyme or reason as to why Cole, who never suffered from allergies, had a fatal reaction. Or for that matter, why he also never got to choose his baby's name. Life could be so unfair. A life that would go on without him.

65

After another grueling funeral within the last six months, Cole Maercker was finally laid to rest. Again, the funeral mass was held at Saint Barnabas in Bellmore and Father Adrian celebrated the mass to a packed church. There were rumors circulating all around town about this third death in this group of friends who had passed way too soon. In very unmistakable ways. Meghan's parents, fearing for her safety as well as their first unborn grandchild's, did not leave her side since the unfortunate passing of their son-in-law. After the incident, Meghan was so grief stricken that she was put on bedrest. As soon as Cole's body was buried, Meghan was given strict orders by Dr. Ferrari that under no circumstances was she to do any physical labor. Her state of mind was too fragile and it was by the will of God that she didn't lose her baby. Her parents saw to this. Her mother pleaded with her to come back home for the time being. Meghan was the oldest of her three other sisters that ranged in age from twenty-two until, her unplanned sister Katie came along who was only ten. Meghan, refused and put up a big argument about them wanting her to move back home for a while. She needed to be where her heart was and where her love for Cole was everywhere she looked at her own home on St. Marks Place. So, with Kimberly's reassurance to Meghan's parents, that she would move in, they did allow her to stay in the house she had shared during happier times with Cole. The first month was the most difficult with Meghan waking up in the middle of the night screaming out for Cole. Kimberly, who slept in the other bedroom, would run in and comfort her, much as Meghan had done for her not so long ago. Kimberly would then take out the small bottles of liquor she had stocked up on from Seaside Liquors in Wantagh, and guzzle them down one after the other, until she passed out not from exhaustion but intoxication.

66

In order to get some semblance back in their lives, from time to time, Kimberly tried to get Meghan out of the house to run some errands. Even if it was just for some fresh air. However, lately it seemed whenever they went complete strangers would stare at them and whisper behind their backs. At first it wasn't too noticeable, but lately it was completely obvious they were the main topic of gossip. Whether it was at the King Kullen Supermarket on Sunrise Highway or the Bellmore Post Office on Merrick Road, people would just stop what they were doing and gape at them. Just last week as they took an evening stroll at Newbridge Park, a couple who Meghan had seen out and about in town, stopped to offer their sympathies for her recent loss. She didn't even respond. It had become so uncomfortable just to leave the house, that Meghan felt like she was becoming a hermit.

67

There was a knock on the front door of Meghan's house. It was late August and she was just two months shy of giving birth. Kimberly had told her she was running an errand. Meghan was sure it was for some more of those tiny liquor bottles she saw buried in the bottom of the trash. She was too exhausted to confront her best friend. After all, Kimberly was a grown woman and should know to make better life choices. She slowly made her way to the front door praying it wasn't her mother or father. Between the two of them, one of them stopped by each day to check on her. Realizing she was still in her bathrobe and slippers at two o'clock in the afternoon, she opened the door and her prayers were answered as it wasn't her parents. Instead it was the next best thing, Father Adrian had come to pay a visit.

68

Meghan was so surprised to see him at her door, that for a minute she forgot to invite him in, "Why, Father Adrian, what a surprise! I mean I wasn't expecting to see you. Oh, please come in." She pointed to her couch and offered him a seat. Graciously he accepted and sat down. Meghan was never a regular Church attendee and often felt guilty about not attending mass every Sunday. Now, as a priest sat on her sofa, she started to feel jittery. Noticing her unease, Father Adrian in his Irish brogue tried to calm her by saying, "My dearest lass, I'm sorry for just stopping by unannounced. I've been meaning to come by and see how you were holding up with the baby coming and all." Meghan, who had gained much more weight than her doctor wanted, wobbled over to the kitchen and took out two bottles of water and proceeded to hand one to Father Adrian, "The best that can be expected at this point. If only my parents would give me some breathing space. It's like they're afraid I'm next."

Father Adrian uncapped the water and took a drink. He didn't know how to proceed with what he was about to say next, "Sorry for just stopping by. It isn't often I make a house call with the busy schedules we have and the lack of priests to fulfill them. They stretch us thin." He took in a deep breath and continued, "Actually, a lot of parishioners have been concerned about the recent events surrounding you and your friends. As I am sworn to secrecy, more than the normal amount are even coming to confession and voicing their worries. A few have known you and Kimberly since you were little girls and after Danielle and now Cole, well................"

Confused as to what he was getting at Meghan asked, "And what are they fearful of if I may ask you Father?"

"My dear girl, even Kimberly's husband whose name has slipped my mind died tragically. And I heard he was a very good surfer and a lifeguard."

"Forgive me Father, but the surfboard came crashing down on his head. Matt's forehead. That's what the autopsy stated. Just an accident."

Father Adrian braced himself for what he was about to add, "Danielle in a car wreck, Cole from an allergic reaction he never experienced before and I even heard, Matt's, yes that was the lad's name, aunt passed horribly. I'm just trying to make sense of it."

Meghan was starting to get irritated at all these accusations. She knew how they all died. Why must he remind her. She plopped down in the recliner next to him and with a bit of an edge in her voice said, "Sense of what Father. If you don't mind me asking. And pardon me, but you're a man of the cloth. You of all people should know these things happen every day."

"I may be a man of the cloth but we're human just like you. I came here in hopes of offering you any guidance I can. Perhaps there is a connection as to why this is all happening."

"A connection. Really Father." Meghan was now losing her composure. "Maybe God saw fit to call my husband and friends back home, before any of them really lived a full life. And now my baby will never know his or her father. Is that a connection or just a God with no compassion."

"God didn't do this work. This was the work of an evil force. Child, I can see I am compromising this situation.

I came here in hopes of opening your eyes to see if there was anything or anyone that you all were involved with. I apologize if I have upset you in any way." Father Adrian rose from the sofa with his water bottle in hand. Meghan pushed off the arms of the recliner and stood as well. Father Adrian took her hand and thanked her again for her time. Before he left, he said a prayer for the safety of Meghan and the delivery of a healthy baby and made the sign of the cross on her forehead. Meghan, who since had calmed, bowed her head as he prayed over her. When he was finished, she too, offered her thanks for the visit, hoping it would be a long time before he would return.

69

Meghan slowly closed the door as she watched Father Adrian get in his car and drive off. What could he have possibly been suggesting she thought. That somehow their deaths were all linked together? Meghan thought it was ludicrous to even go there. They were all accidents, as unfortunate as they were. If only Kimberly were here to listen to this crap she thought to herself as she chuckled. A chuckle that she hadn't had in months. It was probably the last time she and Cole were in that God forsaken restaurant choosing the most awful names for their baby. And in that instant, she felt a quick kick to her ribs. Smiling that her baby was alive and well in her womb, she went about her business, which was to plop herself down in the den and watch mindless shows to keep herself occupied. As she was walking down the hallway that led to the den, she noticed a collage of pictures in a frame on the wall. She stopped to look at it. There were pictures of her and Danielle and Kimberly on the beach in bikinis. Goofy pictures of the six of them on Halloween dressed in silly costumes. The guys with beers in their hands while the girls each held a very large wine glass. Meghan touched her belly. This baby would grow up not only not knowing his or her father but her closest friends too. As tears started to flow down her cheeks caused by her emotional state, she noticed a picture from a ski weekend taken at Hunter mountain four years ago. Kimberly smiling as Matt leaned up against her with his arms crossed. Danielle and Freddie, with his two fingers pointed in a v-shape over her head ruining the picture. Meghan thought that even back then he was always a jerk. And there she and the love of her life Cole were also. Cole's arm around her shoulder, so proud to be her husband. She was his world. He did whatever she asked and never questioned her, she thought. Cole would always see it her way, no matter what. He never ever went against her. Then like a ton of bricks, it hit her. Except for that one time, when they were all gathered at the cabin up in Vermont. The one she rented from the old man Hector Skeeve, a name she didn't think she could ever forget. Cole talking the whole group into keeping that money that Danielle found in the pantry. Cole stating his case as the great lawyer he once was. The money she was dead set against keeping. As she recalled, she was outnumbered by the others in favor of keeping, no better still, stealing what didn't belong to them. One by one, they each voted in favor of taking it. A decision she was not comfortable with. A very wrongful decision. And now as she continued to stare at the group photo, Meghan's tears turned into heartfelt sobs. Three of the six friends were gone including her own husband. And as Father Adrian brought to her attention, in graphic ways in which they had perished. She felt the baby kicking again. Normally, she would be overjoyed, but at this very moment, she had bigger issues at hand. Meghan needed to speak with Kimberly about what needed to be done next. If Kimberly didn't agree, then her life would be in danger. Meghan would see to it that her friend would understand exactly what it entailed. Afterwards, whether he liked it or not, Freddie was next on her agenda. Being the ass he was, Meghan knew he would be anything but agreeable. Meghan now knew that the money was cursed. Somehow it was blood money. Money, she wanted to wash her hands of. Instead of heading into the den as she originally planned, she turned and raced for her phone to call Kimberly. Her decision was made and this time it was final. There was no turning back. If there was a way to turn back the clock, all six of them would still be poor, but at the very least alive.

70

"Okay, okay. Slow down and tell me this theory of yours again. You think the money is what?," Kimberly said after returning back to Meghan's house from the liquor store. Her head was pounding not because Meghan's voice kept repeating itself over and over, but also from the two half pints of Jack Daniels she bought at Seaside Liquors and consumed on the way to Meghan's home.

"Just think about it. When did all these accidents happen? Shortly after we made that stupid decision to take that duffle bag of money and split it up. I'm telling you it all links back to that. Somehow and in some way that money is what is causing all of this. It will continue if we don't give it back. All of what's left of it including getting that miserable prick Freddie on board. Remember, right after Danielle decided to spend some to buy that new car and what?" She answered the question herself. "Danielle died not even two weeks after as she left the dealership for Christ sakes. Then, you guys gave Aunt Mary money to help her out and she dies and….." She stopped before mentioning Matt's name. Besides, Meghan knew Kimberly was half in the bag already and wouldn't remember most of what she was saying. She would have to catch her first thing tomorrow morning, when she first woke up. Even though Kimberly might have a hangover, at least she would be sober enough to let it all sink in. It was also getting late and after the long day Meghan had, including Father Adrian's visit, she too, was ready to call it a night.

Meghan glanced over at Kimberly, who still didn't look the slightest bit convinced. Once again, Meghan tried to make her point to Kimberly and figured she'd give it one last shot by emphasizing on the one word that might truly open Kimberly's eyes. She had said words like tainted, jinxed and blood money but they didn't register the evil she was trying to get Kimberly to see. Kimberly's eyes were glazing over from all the alcohol flowing in her bloodstream. Meghan took hold of her face with both hands, placed each hand on a cheek, and while staring her in the eyes, she said in the most sincere voice she could muster, "That money is CURSED. I'm telling you CURSED!"

71

There was bickering, yelling, and even swearing between the two best friends. They didn't see eye to eye on the money, cursed or not. Kimberly refused to part with her share and said they suffered enough and it was now owed to them. Meghan saw it in a totally different light, so over the next ten days, Meghan did not let up on returning the cursed money. Every chance she got, she told Kimberly what her plan was, until Kimberly finally agreed to take part in it. It was a plan she carefully thought out. It was extremely risky but it had to be done. The money needed to be given back to its rightful owner, even if it meant coming face to face with the disfigured man they stole it from. Labor Day weekend was this coming Saturday. They would make the drive up to Vermont, find the cabin and look for Hector Skeeve. She would make sure to personally hand over the money to him and ask that whatever curse, spell or evil associated with it, be taken away from them. She would plead for his forgiveness for stealing what wasn't rightfully theirs. After that, Meghan prayed their lives would not be threatened and their safety would enable them to live a full life. But as in most cases, life could be a gamble.

72

It was six am and Meghan had already showered and dressed for the drive up to Vermont. She took out the large suitcase she and Cole had hidden their stacks of money in. She lifted it and brought it downstairs. Meghan needed to get Kimberly up and out of bed. She smelled the alcohol on her breath before Kimberly went to bed and surmised that she was once again in a drunken state before she passed out. They still needed to head over to Kimberly's house in West Babylon to get her share. From there they were going to stop at Freddie's apartment in Massapequa. Last week, Kimberly was able to find Freddie's sister's phone number from an old text they had once included her in. She had called Cecilia to make sure he still lived there, and his sister confirmed he did. She also volunteered that Freddie had quit his job after Danielle's accident and had been a recluse ever since. She voiced her concern and asked that if Kimberly did reach out, maybe she could get Freddie to start living again. Kimberly didn't give two shits about Freddie nor did she think she ever would. A leopard can't change its spots. Once an asshole, always an asshole, she thought. All they wanted was his share of the money and he could stay hidden away forever.

73

"Come on already," Meghan said as she shook Kimberly to wake her from her deep sleep. "Jesus, Kimberly, get up or I swear I'm going to pour a glass of water over your face. We need to get going. I want to be back before midnight." At first, Kimberly didn't stir. Then she moaned, flipped onto her side and took a pillow to wrap around her head. Meghan was frustrated as she sat on the edge of the bed, pushed on Kimberly's whole body and she still didn't budge. Meghan got up and walked into the bathroom and took a Dixie cup and filled it with water. She then proceeded to march back into Kimberly's bedroom. She stood over her and tossed the small cup of water directly in her face. Kimberly jumped up from the shock of the water hitting her. She looked dazed until she got her bearings.

"What the fuck Meghan?" She stole a peak at the alarm clock on the night table. "It's like what, six in the morning. Are you for fucking real? Let me sleep a little more. My head is splitting."

Meghan pulled at her nightgown, "We still have to get your money and head over to Freddie. Knowing that jerk, it's going to take a lot of persuading to get him to agree. Please. Get out of bed and let's go. I want this behind us once and for all."

74

By the time Kimberly eventually got up from bed and showered, it was later than Meghan had wanted. When she finally got dressed and they walked out the front door the time was a little after seven thirty. Meghan got behind the wheel of the Yukon, drove north to Sunrise Highway and headed toward the Wantagh State Parkway. Since it was a weekend day, traffic would be light and she would breeze to the Southern State to take her to West Babylon. As she looked over at her passenger, Kimberly looked sleep deprived as she nursed her cup of coffee. With the parkway as empty as it was, they would be there in no time. Kimberly's house was on 11th Street. She was the third house from the end of the block. Or at least it was for the time being.

75

Christine Mafucci was up and out earlier than normal for a Saturday. Being her son was soon starting his senior year in high school right after Labor Day, this would be her normal routine again. She headed over to Stop and Shop and picked up a dozen eggs and a couple of other items to make her family a hearty breakfast. As she was pulling onto 11th Street in West Babylon, she saw Debbie Hyman who lived next store to Mary Quigley's house. For one brief moment, Christine felt a pang of sorrow for both the old woman and her nephew who died so horribly this past year. She also knew that Kimberly was staying at her best friend's house somewhere by Jones Beach on the South Shore. She had heard that her husband had also died suddenly. She thought that some people had really bad luck and was happy she and her family didn't. Christine slowed her car as Debbie Hyman walked from her front door and over to the hedges that separated her home from the Quigley's. Christine, was rather tiny, with strawberry blonde hair and freckles. Debbie Hyman, couldn't look more different with long brown hair and blue eyes like crystals. Noticing that Debbie was just standing there, she rolled her window down as she pulled over by the curb, "Hi Deb, what's going on?"

Debbie waved and said, "Hey, do me a favor. Can you come over after you park? I want ask you something or if it's just me and my imagination."

"Sure thing. I'll be right over. Give me a sec to pull in front of my house." Christine drove her car two houses down and parked the car. She got out with the small bag of groceries and headed over to where Debbie was still standing. "Is everything okay?"

Debbie breathed in a big sniff of air. "Is it me or do you smell something weird coming from the Quigley's? For the last couple of weeks, the odor has been getting stronger. I guess I could call Kimberly but with everything she has been through, I feel terrible to bother her. After all, she's not even been here in the last couple of days if not more."

"Oh my God! My husband Duane just said the same thing. I guess it depends on which way the wind blows. Today the smell isn't that noticeable by us. But at other times, whoa. What do you think it is?"

"To me it smells like sulfur. I googled it just the other day and it stated it could be gas. I was thinking of calling National Grid to report the smell. Better safe than sorry."

"I absolutely agree. That's dangerous not only for this house but look how close our houses are to it. Oh, please, I hope not. You know what? Why don't we both call and report a smell of gas. I know its Saturday and all but let's insist they send a truck out to investigate, just to be on the safe side."

"Perfect, I'll head in now and make the call. I'm just glad it wasn't my nose playing tricks on me. Say hi to Duane for me and enjoy the weekend."

Christine turned around to head home. She decided to make the call first and then start breakfast, letting her family sleep in a bit later. As she walked away she said, "Will do. Say hi to Glenn as well."

76

The customer service representative at National Grid received two phone calls within minutes of one another. Both women complained of smelling gas coming from their neighbor's house. She immediately dispatched an emergency call and a truck was instructed to check out the odor emanating from 2014 11th Street in West Babylon. The driver who received the call was finishing up on another call and said he could be there within a half hour. The customer service representative made a note in her system that he would be there shortly in case they called back to follow up. Unfortunately if they did, it would be too late.

77

Meghan pulled up in front of Kimberly's house, then she opened the passenger door and stepped down from the Yukon. "Give me a few. I just have to grab the money and I'll be right out."

"Ok, but no dilly dallying. Make it fast. We are already behind schedule," Meghan made a point of adding.

Kimberly walked up her walk and unlocked the front door. Instead of heading to where the money was hidden, she went directly into the kitchen and reached down under the sink. She moved a couple of disinfectants and spotted what she was craving. A half pint of Dewar's White Label sat there unopened. She took it out and opened it. She knew that to get through this day, it would take more than this little bottle. Regardless, Kimberly downed the whole bottle in four swigs. Her nerves calmed down almost instantly. Whether or not it was just in her head, it still made her feel better. She tossed the empty bottle in the kitchen receptacle and headed to get the cash. It was exactly where she left it in the hall closet under the snow boots in an attache case that Matt bought because it could be locked. The key was hidden in her snow boot. She reached in and grabbed the key and quickly unlocked the case. Kimberly may have agreed to give back the money but Meghan really had no idea what she had left. Knowing she had no idea of the amount, Kimberly took four stacks and stuffed them into one of Matt's snow boots. She took the attache case and headed for the front door, grateful that she would have money to continue to support her habits. Habits that could be deadly if not stopped.

78

Brett Stevens, the technician at National Grid, called in to let them know, he was just blocks away. He would be there in three minutes in case they were tracking his vehicle, which he knew they were. He had been with the company for twenty-four years and had seen how his freedom was taken away only to be micromanaged. One of his buddies, who also worked there, was specifically told on the sly that all the company trucks were being monitored. There was no more down time to read the paper or take a quick nap. It was strictly business with service call after service call. So, right after he finished the one house, he was on to the next.

79

"Hey, now where are you going? We have what we need. What could you possibly have forgotten," Meghan screamed after Kimberly who dropped the case into the backseat and ran back to the house.

"Please Meghan, just give me a minute. I have to take a fricking pee and I don't want you getting all pissy, if I had to ask you to stop. I promise to make it quick."

"Alright, but please just go and get back in here so we can leave."

80

Brett pulled onto 11th Street and looked at his navigation screen in the truck. It showed 2014 towards the end of the block. He slowed down to see what address number he was currently near and once he saw he was a short distance away, he proceeded to step on the gas.

81

Kimberly had left the front door open purposely. The buzz from the Dewar's had hit her and she needed a cigarette to feel at total ease. Driving for the next four to five hours in Meghan's car and not being able to smoke would be torture. The least she could do was light up a quick one and be on her way.

82

Meghan was slowly losing her patience. For some odd reason, she couldn't help but feel that Kimberly was stalling. She would give her five minutes at most or she would go in and grab her by the hair to pull her out. As she was sitting there fuming, she noticed a National Grid truck approaching. It looked as if the driver was checking to see the house numbers. Meghan counted the seconds. She waited long enough and was going to text Kimberly first to see what the hell was taking so long. She wondered how long it took to take a piss and was getting pissed off herself. Either way if she didn't come out soon enough, she was going to kill her. Not realizing that these were words she would never be able to take back.

83

Kimberly went into the kitchen and placed her handbag on the table. She then reached into her pocketbook and saw what she desperately needed. After all, one cigarette wouldn't kill her. She would have to remember to put a breath mint in her mouth so Meghan couldn't tell she was smoking. With her shaky hand from the effects of drinking a half pint so fast, she took out the pack of cigarettes. Using her other hand, she grabbed her lighter. Kimberly put a cigarette in her mouth, knowing that once it was lit, the first drag was always the best. As soon as she rolled her thumb on the spark wheel, the flame shot up out of the lighter and ignited the gas filled house, blowing it to smithereens. Kimberly never felt a thing.

84

The blast was so powerful and loud, that is shook houses blocks away. The Quigley house was flattened to the ground upon the impact of the explosion. Both the Mafucci's and Hyman's houses were badly damaged with blown out windows and siding ripped off their homes. Luckily, neither family was injured, as they were thrown about their houses from the force of the blast. Pieces of the house flew in many directions, one of which hit the Yukon on the passenger's side door, denting it. Neighbors ran out of their homes to see what had happened. The Mafucci's and Hyman's, also fled their homes, and held onto their children as if their lives still depended on it. Brett, the National Grid technician, pulled up just as the blast occurred, and his front windshield was shattered by a flying object. Having never witnessed something this up close and personal, he called in to his service representative in a quivering voice, that the woman on the other end didn't know with whom she was talking. Brett was thankful that the last visit kept him a bit longer than he expected. After all it saved his life.

85

With all the commotion taking place in that instant, not a single person heard Meghan's wails. She had just finished texting Kimberly, when the whole house exploded, and in a split second was gone. People were running from all directions to get a quick glimpse at the chaos taking place. Sirens were off in the distance as well. Meghan kept screaming and screaming out Kimberly's name, knowing it was useless. Kimberly like the others, including her own loving husband, was now gone too. The tears were spilling down her cheeks as Meghan held onto the steering wheel with her fists tightly clenched around it. She was confused as to what to do next. If she got out of her car, she was going to be held there until the police arrived. They would question her as to why they were there in the first place, and upon closer inspection of her Yukon, they might notice the suitcase and attache case filled with money. That was a chance she wasn't willing to take. Her mind was racing fast and decisions had to be made very quickly. Although her heart was once again shattered, there was nothing she could do to save her last best friend. Meghan forced herself to snap out of it and knew what she must do next. If she even hesitated for the slightest amount of time, it may be too late for her and her unborn child. If she stayed behind, her parents would never let her out their sight and she would be a prisoner in their home. Deep down she also knew that if she didn't continue on her mission, death was soon to catch up with her too. Meghan managed to maneuver the Yukon out onto the street and slowly drove up the block, knowing her next stop would be the most difficult challenge.

86

Meghan was barely able to concentrate on the road, as the tears kept streaming down her face. Twice she swerved into the next lane and had to react quickly, when the other car blasted their horn in warning of a possible collision. Meghan knew her world had fallen apart. It was bad enough losing Danielle and Matt, then the worst of all possible Cole, and now Kimberly too. She was convinced the stealing that money played the biggest role in all these catastrophes. She, now more than ever, needed to get what was left of the cash back to the old man. She blamed herself for not sticking to her guns about leaving the money where she found it. She should have put her foot down and told them all off for even thinking it was okay. After all, she was the most reasonable one of the bunch. The bunch that were now almost all dead. Her life and the life of her child's were presently at stake. She feared the worst was yet to come if the money didn't get back to where and to whom it belonged. Meghan was driving well over the speed limit and the odometer read eighty-five. She immediately put her foot on the brake as she wiped away the tears with the back of her other hand. The last thing she needed was to either be pulled over by a State Trooper, or lose control of the Yukon and plow straight into a tree.

87

Not exactly remembering the route that got her in front of Freddie's apartment at 39 Surrey Lane, she stopped the car. Looking as if she had just woken from a bad dream, Meghan tried her hardest to keep composed as she made her way around the house to the back deck leading up to their door. Freddie and Danielle's apartment was on the second floor of a Cape Style house. They had one bedroom and a kitchen/living room combo, with the bathroom between the two rooms. As Meghan huffed and puffed from the exertion of climbing up the wooden steps, she noticed empty beer cans and fast food bags scattered all over the deck's floor. She assumed that Freddie was just tossing them out the door, instead of putting them in the trash to be taken out. She pushed an empty pizza box with her left foot out of the path and made her way to the door. From the other side, she could hear a television blasting. She was relieved for a brief moment, that Freddie was at least home. She knocked rather loudly at first and waited for him to answer. No one came to the door. She continued to knock again just as loud but called out his name too, "Freddie! Freddie! I know you're in there. I can hear the TV. Please open up. It's Meghan and I need to talk to you." Again, there was no answer. Meghan couldn't stand it anymore and started to plead as she kept banging on the door, "Freddie, please fucking open this door. I swear before God, I'll go grab something and crash it through this window. I mean it. I need your help and I NEED IT NOW!" Panicking that he let her rants fall on deaf ears, she started to look around to see what she could lift and throw through the glass door. There was a snow shovel still out from the past winter laying over by the back of the deck. Meghan decided that would do the trick and was just turning when she saw movement through the glass door. Freddie had gotten up from the sofa and was making his way over. He opened the door and immediately Meghan caught of whiff a putrid smell coming from within. Freddie looked as if he hadn't showered in days or possibly weeks. His dark hair was so greasy it matted to his head. He wore a white v-neck t-shirt that had all sorts of food stains on it. His chest hair protruded out of the t-shirt and needed a manscaping. He wore satin black shorts with white stripes on both sides. His feet were in flip flops and the trail in which he had come was littered about with more garbage than Meghan cared to take notice of. She watched as he stared her up and down before he spoke.

"Bitch, what the fuck do you want?"

Meghan knew he was a jerk but had hoped he may have changed, "Nice way to say hello asshole."

"Knocking on my door like a wild woman. I told you once before to fuck off and I still mean it."

Meghan ignored his rude comment and pushed her way in as she strode past him, into the filth of his apartment. "Listen to me Freddie. Everyone is dead. Do you hear me, DEAD!" Meghan couldn't contain herself any longer and starting crying.

"Easy there. What the fuck are you talking about? My sister told me about Matt and his old fucking aunt, but who else?"

Trying to stop sobbing, Meghan took a deep breathe in and continued, "Everyone you ass, everyone. Cole" She felt her chest constricting from just saying her husband's name and tried to speak but her voice was trembling "...........and......just now......Oh god!.......Kimberly....."

Freddie shook his head as if his hearing was off, "Are you shitting me? Cole and Kimberly. Fuck man! What the hell."

Without asking Meghan, he went over to the sofa and pushed away some take out Chinese containers and sat, "Kimberly and I were coming here to warn you to join us."

"Join you for what?"

Meghan swallowed before continuing, "Listen to me and listen carefully cause I'm only going to say this once. That money we all took is cursed and has to go back. NOW! If we don't…….."

Freddie interrupted her, "No fucking way. I need that shit. In case you haven't noticed, I'm not working. I'm living off of it. So, like I said before, go fuck off."

Meghan couldn't believe he was so curt with her and all at once got hysterical, "Don't you even get what I'm saying you dick. Everyone who touches it or uses it, dies. FUCKING DIES!"

"You're crazy bitch. I've been using it and I'm still here."

"Really and from the looks of it, you probably haven't ventured out in quite some time. I mean look at this filth. It's disgusting. So, tell me. Am I correct?"

Freddie stared at the floor not meeting her eyes.

"Stop ignoring me asshole. Unless you give your share of the money back and come with me right now to do it, you might as well consider yourself warned. Either way I am driving up to that cabin with or without you. If you stay behind be extremely careful spending that cash or who you might give it to. You may feel like you are helping them out, when in reality you are giving them a death sentence." Meghan couldn't hold back as once again she burst into tears, begging one last time, "Please Freddie. I need you to make your decision NOW!"

Freddie paused before answering her. After all, maybe

Meghan was right. He hadn't left his apartment in months, so he has not been in any real danger. His parents as well as his sister and brother would stop over and try unsuccessfully to take him out. One time his kid brother, Carlos, went as far as to pick him up and try to get him out the door. Freddie wriggled free of his grip. He pushed his younger brother out and locked the door. Carlos pleaded with him to let him back in but he refused. He knew Carlos was concerned for his older brother but Freddie didn't budge. Carlos didn't come around after that for weeks. That was until last night when Carlos asked him if he could lend him five thousand for the weekend. One of Carlos' buddies was getting married in two weeks and they were having his bachelor party in Atlantic City, New Jersey. Carlos was working at his construction job in Manhattan, and if Freddie's memory served him correctly, he was leaving right after his shift today at three. Freddie told him to take the money and not to worry about paying him back. Now, if everything Meghan was saying was true, he may have just put his brother's life in danger.

Perhaps it was blood money and because they stole it, they were paying the ultimate price. Their lives for the sake of the almighty dollar. Freddie ran for his cell phone.

88

Meghan watched as Freddie bolted into his bedroom returning with his cellphone in hand. He gestured to Meghan that he needed to make a call first to his brother Carlos at his job. Carlos worked on Saturdays for time and a half. Now, just to be on the safe side, he would give him a call and tell him to burn the fucking money and not give him an argument about doing what he was told.

89

Unlike Freddie, Carlos was a few inches taller at 5'8". Where Freddie had dark hair and eyes, Carlos had taken after his mother, with brown hair and hazel eyes. They didn't even resemble one another in the slightest and often surprised people, when they told them they were brothers. Carlos was pumped up to be going to Atlantic City as soon as his shift was over at three that afternoon. He couldn't believe his best buddy was getting married at only twenty-three, the same age as he was. Carlos wasn't even dating anyone serious, yet alone getting ready to walk down an aisle in matrimony. His foreman on the job had him moving cinder blocks from one end of the construction lot to the other. As he was bending down to grab hold of another block, he felt his cellphone vibrate in his back pocket. Knowing that they weren't allowed to use their phones during working hours, Carlos stole a quick peek to see who was calling. The name came up as his brother Freddie. Carlos thought it odd to receive a call way before noon and especially from Freddie, who hadn't called anyone in the family in months. Ever since his wife Danielle, who Carlos had been very fond of, died in that horrible car accident. Carlos looked around to see where his boss was and then remembered that he was operating the crane, which he happened to be standing under at that precise moment. When he looked up the crane was slowly moving a cement slab the size of a small car directly overhead. Figuring, he was in the best spot not to be seen from where the crane was, he answered the call.

"Carlos, it's me Freddie."

"I know its you bro, your name came up on my display. Why are you calling me this early?"

"Listen to me and listen closely. Where is the five grand I gave you last night?"

Carlos was confused as to why his brother was asking about the money, but answered him, "I left it in my locker on site. It's safe. I have a Master Combination lock on it and besides I hid it in my dirty shirt from the other day. Why are you asking?"

"Because, I need you to do me a huge favor and please don't question me. Go to your locker right this second and take out the money and burn it. Burn it right there and right now! I'm begging you bro."

"Freddie, are you crazy. You fucking gone mad or something. I ain't burning no five fucking thousand. I need that for AC. I have a rooftop pool party planned with bottle service and everything. There'll be bitches hanging all over us. Besides, it's mine and you said I didn't have to pay it back."

Freddie was at his wits end and knew what had to be said to convince his brother, "Listen, the money is not really mine. I stole it. Don't ask. Okay. Bad things have been happening ever since." He choked back his next sentence and forced it out, "Look what happened to Danielle because of that money. I need you to trust me on this and do what I say. BURN the fucking MONEY NOW!"

Carlos had never heard his older brother sound so frantic. He tried to process everything his brother said about stolen money and dying because of it. He started to get freaked out. It was so out of character just listening to his brother ramble on and on that Carlos thought the better of it. If Freddie was that insistent, then he would follow his instructions and go and get the stack of hundreds to burn. He would take it to the side of the site where he knew no one else would be, and light it with the matches he would grab from the office. So, to appease his brother, he would agree to his demands. What he would tell the groom to be, would be another story. One he was dreading.

90

"Thank you for doing this Carlos. I owe you bro and I will make it up to you." Freddie said as he waited for his brother to answer.

Carlos figured he might as well get it over with and do it now. He walked about twenty-five feet, when suddenly there was a loud cracking noise from above, coming from where he was just standing. The cable on the crane that was holding the cement slab snapped and the ton of heavy cement came crashing straight down and landed in the dirt, where Carlos just stood. Co-workers from all over the lot came running over and the commotion was very loud.

Freddie held his ear as close as he could to his phone, trying to hear what had just taken place. He heard voices saying stuff like 'Jesus man you were so lucky' and 'if I were you I would go to Church on my way home today.' Freddie sensed something awful had just occurred and as patiently as he could, waited for his brother to speak.

Carlos was stunned and was in total shock. One his fellow workers ran and grabbed hold of him to move him even further from where the slab had hit the ground. His supervisor jumped off the crane that he was operating and shook him until he got Carlos out of his trance. He walked away from everyone as they were still talking about the incident. Carlos then realized he was still holding his phone and spoke into it with a very shaken up voice, "Freddie, I almost got flattened by a piece of cement. Bro, maybe you are right after all. That was the closest call I hope to ever experience in my life. EVER! After it quiets down over here, I give you my word that money is going up in flames. And trust me, no one is putting it out."

91

Freddie couldn't believe what his brother had just confirmed. A cement slab would have crushed his brother to death if he hadn't taken those few steps to do what his brother had asked. And all because of that money that Meghan said needed to be returned. He now believed her theory of the curse. There was no denying it anymore. If Freddie wanted to live, then the the money had to go.

92

Meghan watched and even tried to listen and eavesdrop on the one-way conversation Freddie was having. As the two brothers conversed, something bad must have taken place. Meghan saw Freddie's face go completely pale. And then Freddie kept saying over and over, 'Carlos talk to me. What is going on?' What felt like an eternity before Carlos did reply, then made Freddie look even worse. His usually tanned complexion turned even whiter. And as soon as he hung up the phone, Meghan knew he was now rearing to go.

Part IV

THE OUTCOME

93

Meghan who usually let Cole do most of the driving, drove the entire trip up to West Dover, Vermont. With her adrenaline at an all-time high, they only made two pit stops for gas and mostly to relieve her bladder. They entered the town at four-thirty that afternoon. Meghan had wanted to be there earlier but was thankful Freddie had believed her and made the trip as well.

Freddie, looked down at his phone, since it had the best GPS, and said, "The third right after this light. That's the road we take up to the cabin. And what do we do once we get there? Just knock on the fucking door and say, 'hey fuck face, yeah you with the deformed face.' Here's your fucking money back not take back this…." He thought for the appropriate choice of word, "curse, yep, that's it. Take back this fucking curse, you ugly old piece of shit man."

"Please Freddie, be nice. Bad enough he looks like that, don't say it aloud. And PLEASE don't say anything to his face."

"Who's to say he will even be there. What do we do if he's not? Search high and low. I say we just leave the money on the table in the kitchen with a note and split."

"Let's cross that bridge when we come to it. Until then, just keep leading me in the right direction."

94

The Yukon pulled up in front of the cabin. What had once looked like a peaceful log cabin, now had a more sinister appeal. Meghan with much effort, lowered herself out and down off the running board. Freddie came around and helped her by taking hold of her hand and walking her to the front porch steps. Meghan couldn't believe there was an ounce of kindness in Freddie but thanked him just the same. He had at least made the effort. Thinking back to that first day, when their lives were still intact, and life was pretty dam good, Meghan became anxious. She felt her stomach flip and didn't know if was the baby or her nerves. Meghan asked Freddie to get the key under the rocker, crossing her fingers it was still there. As luck would have it, the key was in the exact same spot, as if it had never been touched. As she opened the lock, Freddie scooted back to the truck and grab the three different containers, each with their share of money. Awkwardly, he made his way up and followed her into the cabin. As soon as he stepped in, he placed them on the floor. Meghan went over to the lamp and turned the switch. The light went on, which meant that maybe Hector was somewhere around. She assumed the power would be off but that may have meant he was here not too long ago. Either in the house or on the property. Meghan called out his name, "Mr. Skeeve, are you here? Please if you are, come out." Her voice was hysterical now, "Please, please, please...................We have your money. We want to give it back. BACK! Come......out.........." Freddie searched the three bedrooms also calling out his name in the process. There was no answer. Meghan realized she should have called and tried to speak with Hector Skeeve, before making the trip up here. She figured there was no use punishing herself now. Either way, they were leaving the money. She went in the kitchen and started going through the drawers for some paper and a pen. After Freddie searched around the grounds still yelling out Hector's name to no avail, on her say so, he went into the pantry and pulled out the original duffle bag, that contained this wretched cash.

95

As Meghan finished writing her plea for forgiveness, Freddie stuffed the money back into the duffle bag. Noticing Meghan wasn't looking at him and was concentrating on what she wrote, he took one stack and stuffed it in the front of his jeans. Surely one pack wouldn't be missed, and as far as the 'curse', he would take the risk. It was a shame to give the whole thing back. One measly little stack of bills, wouldn't cause any harm. He made sure it was well hidden, then placed the bag back into the pantry. Apparently, Freddie wasn't thinking straight, it was only hours before, his kid brother almost suffered a fatal accident, over just a small sum of five thousand. Freddie should have learned his lesson, a lesson that could cost him dearly.

96

Meghan was devastated that Hector was nowhere in sight, and as Freddie helped lift her back into the driver's seat, she couldn't stop crying. She was worried that Hector Skeeve wouldn't come back to this cabin for quite some time. Time that was ticking away, time that was truly wasting. Time, she felt they didn't have. Meghan started the Yukon and made a u-turn to head back down the road. She looked at the gas gauge and saw the needle at the quarter of a tank. They would need to stop at the gas mart in town and fill up before they left. She also needed to use the facilities, since the baby was pressing on her bladder. She could have peed inside the cabin, but it now felt eerily haunted and the further away from it the better she felt.

97

Hector Skeeve had heard a car off in the distance and made a mad dash for the back door. The two other couples weren't expected to arrive until after seven thirty, so he couldn't imagine who would be coming up this early. Hector made his way into the backyard and hid behind a thick tree for cover. A few minutes later, he heard a woman's voice calling out his name followed shortly by a man's doing the same. He stood still and didn't make a sound. These voices sounded frantic. Trying to steal a quick glance, all at once the backscreen door swung open, and out came a short stocky young guy. Hector rubbed his eyes. He couldn't quite put a finger on who this guy was, until the guy called back to Meghan, saying no one was in the backyard either. Once Hector heard the name Meghan, he recognized the fat little guy. They were those three couples that came up here this past winter to use the cabin to ski. Meghan was the girl who spoke with him over the phone to make the arrangements. The ones who stole the cursed money. Hector smiled at that thought. Still uncertain as to why they had come to pay him a visit, he hid deeper behind the tree. The whole ordeal lasted about thirty minutes at most, when suddenly he heard the car start and drive off. Slowly he made his way back into the cabin. As soon as entered the kitchen, he noticed a letter left under a vase. Instantly he had a flashback of another note he had once read from years ago. It was from his son Nathaniel, bidding him a final farewell. It was the last time Hector ever saw the son he missed so much. Hector picked up the paper and started to read it.

Hello Mr. Skeeve,

I hope you will remember me. More, I was hoping you were here so I could do this in person. Face to face. My name is Meghan Maercker and my husband Cole and I along with two other couples rented your cabin this past Martin Luther King weekend.

He stopped reading as he saw what looked like a wet stain at that given spot. He read on.

We did something unspeakable. We took a very large amount of money that was hidden in a duffle bag in your pantry from you. It didn't belong to us and we stole it. I am so sorry we did that and if I could turn back time, I would have made sure we never touched the money.

Hector knew what was coming next. He could just feel it in his bones. A smile even crossed his face. He continued to read.

You see, accident after accident has taken the lives of four of us and even one of my friend's aunts. Anyone who came across this money. I don't know how or why, but I know it has some sort of spell, or I hate to use this word, curse, associated with it. We, meaning Freddie and I, are the only two left. I lost my husband shortly after finding out I was pregnant. Now I fear for my life and my unborn child's. We gathered up most of the money and have placed it back in the duffle bag and returned it to the pantry where we first stumbled upon it. We want to give it back and say we are truly, deeply sorry. We also want you to take away whatever it is that has caused all these horrors in our lives. I want to live and I want my baby to live and grow up to live as well. Please Mr. Skeeve forgive us for we know we have sinned. Find it in your heart to break the spell and let us be. I ask you this through Christ our Lord.

All I ask is to let me LIVE,
Meghan Maercker

Hector finished reading the letter and crumpled it in his hands like he did the other from his son. It was really not up to him who lived or died. After all the curse was placed on him from the old woman. Ed's mother. He never touched it in all these years, and knew that it would bring nothing but bad fortune to those who did. He did, in fact, like the girl named Meghan. She was the sweetest of the whole lot. The one she called Freddie he despised. He was the nastiest of the bunch. Figures he would still be alive. Hector imagined that since the money was rightfully returned, maybe the twist of fate would leave them be. He could only hope. He put this behind him for now. Knowing that soon the others would arrive, Hector did a once over around the place to make sure all things were in order. As he was told, from the realtor since he no longer wanted to speak to the renters directly, these young folks were coming up to do some apple picking. Hector at first did want to be gone before they came, but changed his mind. His mind that was getting warped from age. He decided to wait around for them to arrive and see how they would react to his appearance. A little game of fate. Either they would be sympathetic or find him pathetic. This time he would be ready for either. He strolled back into the kitchen and opened the pantry door. Because he was old and fragile, it took all his effort to drag the duffle bag out so it was more visible in the pantry. Instead of closing the door, he left it wide open so the bag could be seen. As he walked back to the living room to take the same spot as he did months ago, a smile spread from cheek to cheek across his face. He was looking forward to this new game of destiny. Be nice or be dead. The decision would be all theirs to make.

98

"There up on the left, pull in there for gas," Freddie instructed Meghan.

"I won't be long. A quick trip to the ladies room. Do you think you can you pump the gas?"

"Of course, I may be a dick but a guy can't let a fully pregnant woman pump her own gas. Besides, I want to grab a few snacks for the long haul back."

Meghan didn't reply but only smiled, glad Freddie realized that he was a dick. She walked towards the mini-mart just as a Subaru outback pulled alongside the gas pump next to theirs. Two younger girls jumped out and rushed in before her. They ran straight to the bathroom. Meghan was so mad she let them beat her in. After she paid the cashier for the gas, she went over to the snack displays. She wished she was quicker, but in her condition, she couldn't walk any faster. While she waited, she decided to look for a couple of treats for herself. They were taking forever. Freddie had since filled the tank, adjusted the stack of money that was sliding out from his underwear, and came into the store himself. He was walking over to Meghan when the bathroom door burst open and the two giggling girls came out. One of them was saying something about who rents a cabin from a person with a name like Skeeve. Both Meghan and Freddie looked at each other with a note of panic on their faces. Meghan couldn't help but blurt out, "Excuse me, but did you just mention the name Skeeve? Are you heading up to his cabin?" The girls stopped their silly giggling and were deciding whether or not to answer this stranger, one who looked about ready to pop out a baby, they stole a glance at Freddie too. Both Meghan and Freddie looked absolutely horrible. Like they had been to hell and back. The girls walked quietly past them and tried to remain silent as they did. Meghan needed to know if they were staying at the cabin. She turned around and stood in front of them blocking their path, "Listen, I know I look like a crazy woman but please tell me. I'm only going to ask. Did you rent that cabin from a Hector Skeeve?" The two girls didn't know what to say. They remembered reading his name on the contract and one of their boyfriends actually laughed out loud just at the sound of it. Meghan took another step closer and fear was evident in their eyes. Freddie took a hold of her arm and pulled her back to let them pass. The girls who were afraid and just wanted to be in the presence of their boyfriends, rushed past, but not before one of them yelled back, 'Yes. Why, is there something we should know?'

99

The boyfriends looked over at Freddie and Meghan deciding if they wanted to confront them, but at the urging of their girlfriends, decided against it. Freddie's appearance only scared the girls more. They all got back into the Subaru and started to drive off.

100

Freddie knew by just looking into Meghan fearful eyes what he need to do next. He wanted to warn the two young couples that if Hector was there, to treat him with kindness. Also, if they stumbled across the duffle bag to leave it alone. Even if Freddie had to rant and rave like a crazy man, he would mention where they were from and tell the couples to google their last names to see what had happened to them for stealing the cash. He pushed open the door as Meghan desperately tried to follow. The Subaru put on its blinker and pulled out onto the road. They didn't see Freddie as he ran after the car. They had already forgotten the incident and lit up a joint to pass around. Meghan had just ran past the pumps and watched as Freddie ran right out in the road, and directly in front of an eighteen wheeler barreling down on him, Meghan screamed out Freddie's name but it was too late. The driver of the truck didn't even see him as he drove over him and flattened him to the ground. The only saving grace was that Freddie didn't see what hit him from behind as he too was yelling out to the couples to turn around before it was too late. Little did Freddie realize it was way too late for him.

101

Everything happened in slow motion as Meghan first noticed the truck a split second before it took Freddie's life. The truck driver hit the brakes as soon as he realized he struck someone and was a distance up the road. Hundred dollar bills floated up into the air. The cashier came running out screaming in his phone for 911 to send help. Meghan fearing to look over at his body, hesitantly glanced in the direction, covering her eyes between her fingers. As Meghan peeked through her fingers, it was in that very instant, she noticed the money that swirled all around the pavement. She started to wobble back and forth. Her vision was getting blurry. Images of Danielle and Kimberly with Matt, along with her beloved Cole flashed before her eyes. She tried to steady herself, but her whole body was swaying. Dizziness was fast approaching, and her first thought was she really needed to release her bladder. But before she could even make the effort, she fainted. As she hit the ground, thankfully on her side, it wasn't her bladder that let go, it was her water that broke.

102

Meghan started to regain consciousness. She opened her eyes to a brightness that blinded her and made her close them again. This time she slowly opened them, so they could adjust to the light. Meghan was groggy as she tried to lift herself up. She couldn't recall what had happened at first. She racked her brain for any inkling as to what had happened, when it suddenly dawned on her. A mental image appeared and it was of a truck running down Freddie. Freddie was dead just like the rest of them. Meghan was the only one left. She and her unborn baby. She gently went to pat her baby bump. Her stomach was no longer as huge as it was. Meghan sprung up, with her arms flailing, and let out the most death defying scream most people in their lifetime had ever heard.

103

Two nurses rushed into the room and took hold of her arms, restraining her as a man in a suit followed in shortly afterwards. The man quickly took hold of her arms, releasing the nurses from doing so and gently placed them at her sides. While trying to soothe her, he then took his hands and pushed her hair back off her forehead. Meghan didn't recognize her surroundings but from what she could tell she was in some sort of a hospital in a bed. This man now sitting on the edge of her bed, spoke to her softly for the next few minutes. Meghan wasn't fully comprehending all he said. She felt like she had been through her own hell. She did notice that the man looked to be in his late fifties to early sixties with a full head of gray hair. The thing that struck her most about him was there looked to be some kind of sadness in his eyes. They appeared to be of a dull blue color. She couldn't help but think that when he was younger, his eyes must have been one of his best features. Even as he smiled at her reassuring her all was fine, there was an emptiness to them. Before, she could muster up the strength to speak, the man did just that, "Rest assured Mrs. Maercker, you and your baby are perfectly fine."

Meghan rubbed her belly and started sobbing. The man took her hand and continued, "They rushed you into the hospital after the ambulance found you on the ground by the mini mart." He didn't mention the other events that followed with the death of what he supposed was a friend or the possible father of the baby, since the identification on the deceased was of a Freddie Torres. Your water had broken and you went into active labor shortly after. We rushed you into the delivery room and it was there that I delivered a healthy baby boy.

Meghan's mouth was parched but she whispered, "But I wasn't due for another four weeks. Is, oh my God, he ok?"

"I didn't realize you were a few weeks early." He carefully chose his next words, "I guess with the passing of your boyfriend that you witnessed, forced you into premature labor. Your son is getting the best care and is currently in Neonatal care. He weighed in at a healthy 6 pounds and 11 ounces. He would have been a real bruiser if you went full term."

Meghan couldn't believe what she was hearing. Her SON was healthy and weighed a nice six plus pounds. Confused at the moment, by the name Freddie Torres and his association as the father, Meghan felt the need to clarify the situation, "Oh, no sir. That wasn't my son's father. You see my husband passed a few months back. He died…..."

The man interrupted her, "Oh I'm so sorry to hear that." Trying to make sense of all this, between her husband's recent death and now this other man's brutal demise, he wanted to change the subject. "Did you and your husband have a name for your child?"

Meghan hesitated as she stared at this man, who she now assumed helped delivery her son, but wanted to confirm, "Pardon me for asking, but you did deliver my baby?"

He raked his hand through his own hair as he answered,

"But of course. I was the doctor on call and was happy that I was there to bring this little guy into the world. I only wished it were under happier circumstances. Again, I'm sorry about your husband. If it is any consolation, my very own mother died giving birth to me."

Meghan, for some odd reason, felt bad for this man. The doctor who brought her son into the world and gave him life. Bad enough for a child, very much like her own, not having his father, but a child without its mother was unimaginable. She felt pity for him. Now trying to change the subject herself, she remembered that he asked her if they had name for her son picked out. Unfortunately, they never did pick either a boy or girls' name. Suddenly, she was curious as to this doctor's name was since he did indeed bring her baby boy into the world. Then Meghan realized what she hoped would be true. That this world could now be a safe haven for her and her son, where they could now be safe since she did return the cursed money. Pushing the thought away that it could be anything else, she asked, "I'm sorry I never did get your name doctor. Perhaps I can name him after you. I was supposed to give birth and my OBGYN was a woman. Doctor Joanne Ferrari, so that wouldn't work in his case."

The doctor looked puzzled but then a smile crossed his faced as he would be honored to have a child named after him. He and his wife were unable to conceive any children of their own. They spent countless hours and visits with many doctors over the years only to eventually be told that his sperm wasn't viable for reasons never fully determined. For years, they tried and it wore them both out. His wife, after ten years of what he thought was a happy marriage, it wasn't truly the case. Although they travelled to the most beautiful places all over the world and wined and dined at all the best restaurants, it wasn't enough. They both wanted what they lacked. A family of their own. Since he couldn't give her what she wanted most, she secretly ran off and left him for a male nurse. Last he had heard, she was living somewhere in San Diego, and had a boy and two girls over the years. He did continue as a OBGYN and delivered his fair share of babies in his career. It always brought him much joy when he saw the happiness a new born baby gave to parents. Whether it was their first or fourth, each baby was given a love like no other. His only regret was he would never experience that firsthand. He did, after all, blame himself for something he did so many years ago. He had never forgiven himself for not just losing his wife, but for what he gave up to be with her. He lived many years carrying that burden, but could never ever face the person he did it to. He shook his head, now noticing this young mother was waiting for an answer, as he got his bearings back and replied, "I'm sorry. I was lost in thought for a moment. Even daydreaming for a brief second. My first name is Nathaniel. As my own father reminded time after time, it means something like a Gift from God. He always said that was what I was with my mother passing as she gave birth to me. That, I was, a special gift left behind for him. From the moment I was born, even my father who daily had to deal with a badly disfigured face from a fire, worshipped the ground I walked on. If only I did right by him." Nathaniel felt embarrassed as he tried to stop a tear from falling down his cheek. He wiped at it quickly, hoping the young mother didn't see it.

Meghan had stopped listening to the doctor as soon

as he said his name was Nathaniel. Her only thought was where she had heard that name before. Even the gift of God came jumping out at her. But now she could not remember. It wasn't as if the name was a common name like Michael or John. She concentrated just on the name Nathaniel. She kept repeating over and over in her head. Then Nathan popped into her head and a sudden scenario came to be. She remembered reading a card left in a drawer in the bedroom of that cabin. Cole had called her a busybody for snooping. The night she and Cole made love like they never had before. The night she was sure she got pregnant. Meghan wondered if it could be just a coincidence and took a deep breath before asking the one question she feared most. "Doctor Nathaniel, I'm sorry but what……" She stopped as she started to feel like she was going to hyperventilate. It took all she had to say the next four words, she so dreaded to ask, "is your last name?"

Baffled by this question from this new young mother, who only moments ago wanted to give her son his name, the doctor kindly answered, "My name is Nathaniel Skeeve. Doctor Nathaniel Skeeve. Why, do you know………" He never finished what he was about to say. You see, Meghan Maercker, once again screamed out words he was sure never to forget.

"Nooooooo, it can't be. Please any NAME but that!" Hearing the doctor, moments ago, say his father was disfigured, confirmed her worst fear. Frightening images of the badly burned face of his father, Hector, flashed before her eyes. This was no coincidence. Again, Meghan felt like she was being tested, and it was too much for her to bear. She wondered if the nightmare would ever end. Meghan continued to scream out. Taking hold of her hand and trying to calm her down, Nathaniel continued to reassure all would be fine. She pulled her hand from his. His soothing words fell on deaf ears as she once again fainted. It would be hours before she would be coherent enough to be able to see her new baby boy. The son she would name anything but Nathaniel. Later on, when Meghan was stable enough, a Gift from God or not, her decision would be made. As it would turn out, her son would never have anything or any association with a name of Skeeve. That was one promise Meghan knew she would always keep.

EPILOGUE

THREE YEARS LATER

Meghan watched as little Jack came running from his room and jumped up on her bed, "Mommy, mommy, we move today? I miss house."

Jack had just turned three. Her family as well as Cole's whole family were there to help celebrate his birthday last week. Meghan thought it unreal, the resemblance Cole's son had to his father. With sandy brown hair and the lightest blue eyes, it was like looking at a miniature version of the husband she would always miss.

Back on that fateful day, her father and mother had driven up to Vermont the moment they got the call about their daughter having gone into labor. After arriving at the hospital and being told of the passing of Freddie Torres, her mother had not left her side for many months to come. Rumors of the tragedies that five of the friends had suffered, had since quieted down. At first, national attention from local media and news stations had wanted an exclusive interview. Surely something must have led to the accidental deaths of each of them so closely together, and the networks were eager to obtain the rights. Her parents refused any offers and stuck to their guns that their daughter had suffered enough and needed time to heal and recuperate. If and only when their daughter was able to share her experiences would they allow it, knowing full well, Meghan would never grant anyone her permission. There wasn't enough money or money she had wanted, for her to share the truth behind it. She felt it better to leave it in her past and never recall the events. Eventually bigger news came along and hers slowly drifted away never to resurface into the limelight.

Years had passed and life was good for Meghan and little Jack as he continued to grow into a toddler and now a little boy. Gone was the fear that anything else bad would happen to her or her child. Meghan had prayed that by giving back that cursed money, it would somehow save their lives. The only regret was that she no longer wanted to stay in the house that she and Cole tried to make their home. Everywhere she looked there were memories too painful for her to push away. Ironically enough, when Cole found out he was going to be a father, he took out a million-dollar insurance policy shortly before his death. Ten months later Meghan received the hefty check from the Life Insurance company. Meghan wanted to live a simple life and remain in Bellmore to be close to her and Cole's families, where she felt safe. Another reason was because the school district was still very good and would provide Jack with an excellent education. She listed her house on the market and it sold within three weeks. The closing had taken place yesterday. Today, the movers were on their way and the house she purchased on Prospect Place was just a few blocks away. It was a cute extended cape on a dead end, where she knew her son could play out on the street safely when he got older. She would wait for the movers to arrive and instruct them on what needed special care when handling. Then she would head over to her cute little house where her siblings and parents were to help her unpack and get settled in. You see, Meghan was very excited for this new chapter in her life. There would always be times when she would miss her best girlfriends and shed many tears for them, since their lives were cut so short. Cole, on the other hand, would be her most painful loss. As it was now, a day had not gone by where she didn't smell his cologne or feel his presence around both herself and Jack. She had hoped those feelings would never stop.

The two movers had arrived precisely at the time promised. After they exchanged what was needed, Meghan scooped little Jack in her arms, and headed to the front door. She walked out into a beautifully sunny day. She looked up, and the sky was crystal clear with not a cloud to be seen. For a brief second she thought of Danielle, Kimberly, Matt and Cole and knew they were all her guardian angels. They would all look after her and Jack for as long as they both lived. She smiled knowing they were all in heaven. Meghan then hugged Jack even tighter, as she once thought she would never have lived through the hell of that one treacherous year.

LATER ON THAT SAME DAY

The movers had packed most of the furniture and loaded it into the moving truck. There were just a couple of more smaller pieces to haul downstairs and they were ready to drop off everything not even a quarter of a mile away. It was an easier day than they thought. This lady wasn't a hoarder and there weren't that many boxes they had to pick up. Moe and Jimmy loved days like these. If they finished with enough time left over, they could head to the local bar and down a few beers before going home. Moe, the bigger of the two at 6'4", was African American, while Jimmy was from El Salvador and a full six inches shorter. Moe was thirty-one and Jimmy was twenty-nine. Both of them were single with no serious girlfriends. They had been with the same moving company for the past seven years and enjoyed working with one another. They each had a mutual respect for one another and were friends on the outside. The owner of the company knew of their friendship, and let them work most jobs together, as there were never any complaints from the customers regarding them. No items ever went missing and nothing was damaged on their shift. Jimmy climbed the stairs and went into Meghan's bedroom. There was one nightstand left to be loaded onto the truck. He bent to lift it since it was light for him. Jimmy worked out seven days a week and was quite muscular. He lifted it up and as he was turning around, something underneath caught his eye. There appeared to be two very large stacks of money rubber banded tightly together. Jimmy shouted out for his best buddy to come into the room. He didn't hesitate to even think of keeping it for himself. If anything, he was pumped to let Moe see his find. And from what it looked like, a killing was more opt of a term for this amount of cash. Moe walked in to see Jimmy waving two stacks of cash in his face. After counting the large amount of money and jumping up and down like they hit the jackpot, they had a decision to make. Do they tell the young mom of the money they discovered or just not say anything and keep it? Apparently, someone else must have stashed it there and she was totally unaware that it existed. Moe and Jimmy had visions of living the good life for a while. At least for one weekend in Las Vegas. The best champagne and the hottest girls around. Knowing at that precise moment, that a soon planned trip to Vegas would be booked, they wanted to unload the contents of the truck as fast as possible. They made a pact to keep it a secret and not say a word to the woman. If down the line, she did remember, which they were almost positive she wouldn't, they would simply deny it. Their boss would believe them since their records were impeccable. For now, the decision was clearly made. It was theirs to keep. Moe and Jimmy would rush to get the job done. After all, it was Friday and they could still pull off getting a flight out west for the weekend. So, as they got into the moving truck and pulled away, happy thoughts pranced in their heads. Early tomorrow morning Jimmy would pick up Moe and off they would go to the airport to catch a flight. What they didn't realize was that Jimmy's back axle had broken, when he hit that rather large pothole the other day. Right after, as he accelerated, he felt the whole car vibrate but pushed it from his head. He didn't have money for a car repair. Jimmy also chalked the vibrations up to the fact that he liked to speed. Tomorrow morning, he would be given that chance again. He would oversleep, wake up late and have to make up for time, if they were to catch their flight and get to spend the newly found money. As any mechanic would have informed Jimmy, if they inspected his car on a lift, speeding with a broken axle could be very deadly. Just how deadly, both Jimmy and Moe had no idea, but would find out soon enough. Early the next morning, as Jimmy drove twenty miles over the speed limit, the axle would finally split, causing Moe and Jimmy to look over at each other just as.........................the cursed money came back into PLAY!

Thank you so much for reading and I hope you enjoyed it! I would truly appreciate you leaving a quick review on Amazon. If you'd like to reach out to me my links are below:

www.facebook.com/vincentscialobooks
vscialo@gmail.com

Also by Vincent N. Scialo

The Rocking Chair

Randolph's Tale (A Journey for Love)

Deep in the Woods

Heigh-Ho

Not by Choice

Jesus (Journey Every Step Un-Sure)

ABOUT THE AUTHOR

This is an exhilarating much anticipated seventh novel for Vincent N. Scialo. Unlike his previous six novels, this story will having you turning the pages to read the explosive conclusion to what will happen to these three young couples and the decision they chose to make. His novels The Rocking Chair and Randolph's Tale (A Journey for Love) still receive much acclaim and to this very day are sold at the Washington D.C. Holocaust Museum. They are still much talked about among many book clubs today. For those who crave the ultimate in horror and suspense, a taste of Deep in the Woods will leave you speechless. This novel is sure to keep you up late at night with the lights on. And if you ever wondered what lives the seven little men led before meeting the purest of snow, Vincent offers a dark fabled fairytale. Heigh-Ho is for the young at heart still in love with classic bed-time stories. Not by Choice will grip you from start to finish as this medical suspense has the reader rooting for the main character throughout the story. Lastly, for your spiritual side, JESUS (Journey every step un-sure) lets you experience what it would be like to walk the four seasons with Jesus at your side. Vincent continues to perfect his work while residing in Bellmore, Long Island, with his wife Jennifer and his son Jeff. His daughter, Marissa, recently wed and now lives in Massapequa.

Printed in the United States
By Bookmasters